Nasha
THE FIRST DOG

MICHAEL MILONE

michael milone

ARENA PRESS
NOVATO, CA

For information about ordering additional quantities, contact:
Arena Press (a division of Academic Therapy Publications)
20 Commercial Blvd., Novato, CA 94949
(800) 422-7249

ISBN: 978-1-57128-517-1

10 09 08 07 06 05 04 03 02 01

Printed in the U.S.A.

*To the countless
children of the first dog,
who have loved
and protected
humans for
a thousand generations*

Chapter 1

The wolf pup nestled in Maddia's arms. She looked at the girl with loving eyes as she snuggled into a more comfortable position. The tiny wolf paid little attention to the humans surrounding her in the hut made of animal skins, tree limbs, and branches. All the pup knew is that she was safe and warm.

"Leave the wolf pup where you found her. We do not have food enough for ourselves, let alone a wolf pup. The wolf has been our enemy since the beginning. If you do not return the wolf to where she was, I will take it from you and will leave it far from our camp where you will not find it. I will not be happy to do so, but it is my duty."

Baratho made his declaration from a position of authority. He had been leader of the clan for many seasons. He sometimes appeared harsh, but he had guided the clan through difficult times. Baratho was a good hunter and rarely came home with empty

1

hands. What is probably more important is that he made sure that the clan's food was distributed to every person, not just those who had been in the hunt. The members of the clan respected his skill as well as his fairness.

With an inner strength beyond her years, Maddia stood tall. She held the wolf pup to her chest and said softly yet defiantly, "I will not abandon her."

"You must," snarled Gortush, his gravelly voice filled with displeasure. "Baratho has said so."

The words of Gortush came as something of a surprise to all who heard them. He and Baratho were at odds, and those assembled in the hut believed that he would kill Baratho if given a chance. Gortush was a coward, however, and would never challenge Baratho in a fair contest.

Gortush proceeded, viewing Maddia and the pup with disgust. "We should send both the girl and the wolf pup away and let the animals take care of them. All of us will be better off without them."

No one in the hut stirred. The air was so still that those who had assembled were afraid to breathe and break the quiet. Then a familiar voice spoke.

"The wolf pup will alter our world in extraordinary ways. Maddia should not abandon her. I see our lives bound together for all eternity. The Great Spirit has entrusted to us a gift. It is true that the wolves have always been our enemies, but that will change. The wolf will be a friend to humankind for as long as there are days."

Lartha placed the end of her staff cautiously on the ground and rose to her feet. Even though she had lived many years, more than anyone could count, the healer of the clan possessed considerable power. With her words, the fates of Maddia, the pup, and humans were forever entwined.

With a nod toward Lartha, Baratho said, "You may keep the wolf pup, Maddia. I do not understand how Lartha arrived at this conclusion, but I trust that what she says will come to pass. From this day onward, you are responsible for the wolf pup."

Despite trying to disguise his feelings, it was with some relief that Baratho permitted Maddia to keep the wolf pup. He was not an unkind man, and he had a fondness for Maddia. Baratho felt kinship with the animals that shared their world, and like most of the clan, he would kill an animal only for food or to save a human. He would have been saddened if he had to force Maddia to leave the pup.

"Thank you, Baratho," whispered Maddia. Her defiance instantly turned to elation and gratitude, and she bent her head slightly so no one would see the tears that welled in her eyes.

"You may rejoin your family, Maddia. I hope that Lartha's words are correct, and that the pup will grow up to be part of our clan."

As she walked out of the hut, Maddia saw Gortush glare at Lartha and then at her and the wolf pup. *He is not much of a warrior if he considers it necessary to threaten an old woman, a girl, and a wolf pup*, she thought to herself.

Chapter 2

The story of the wolf pup had begun a few days earlier. Maddia, her younger brother Lakus, and her older cousin, Ganni, were searching for the special stones used for tools and axe blades. They were not far from the clan's camp on a level stretch of barren ground at the base of a steep ridge. The boys worked the area near the middle of the plain, while Maddia stayed closer to the ridge.

The growl that Maddia heard was low and quiet, causing the girl to become transfixed. She was positive the sound came from a wolf, but she could not see it. All of them were in serious danger if wolves were close enough for her to hear them.

Lakus and Ganni were a short distance away. She waved her arms frantically and signaled to them to come to her. She did this silently using hand gestures that the clan members knew. The two boys were in a situation where they had no cover, and the wolves would be likely to attack them first. Maddia was by a cliff that would offer them at least a small measure of sanctuary.

"What is it, Maddia?" asked Ganni when he reached her, breathing heavily from the run. Although a boy, he was bigger and stronger than many men. When groups of children were foraging for edible plants or other things, Ganni went with them as a guard.

"I heard a wolf growl, but I cannot see where it is. I did not want the two of you to have no place to seek protection if more wolves came by." Maddia scanned the area nervously but saw no wolves.

"But we looked around before we came down from the hill," said Lakus. "We did what we were supposed to, did we not? How could we have missed the wolves?"

"Yes, we did what we should have," answered Ganni, "but the wolves might have made their way here while we were hunting for the tool stones. We should go back to the camp."

"Wait," insisted Maddia. "There it is again."

All three of them heard the sound this time, but they could not see its source anywhere. Glancing behind her, Maddia saw a wolf pup in the opening of a deep hole in the rocky wall. It had probably been drinking from a spring when it saw them.

After growling and baring its teeth, the tiny pup crawled weakly into the den. Normally, Maddia, Ganni, and Lakus would have returned to camp. Nothing was more dangerous for a human than to encounter a wolf pup. Almost always, the mother or

5

the whole pack would be nearby. But the three of them had been watchful before they came down from the cliff to the flat ground to scour the area for the tool rocks. There was no evidence that wolves had been there for days. Believing that the pack had gone, Maddia became worried about the pup.

"I will give the pup some meat," said Maddia. "Continue looking for signs of wolves."

"Are you sure you want to do that?" asked Ganni. "We do not know where the pack is. They could appear at any time."

Maddia didn't wait for Ganni to complete what he was saying. She hastened to the small cave and got down on her hands and knees. Very slowly, she pulled a piece of dried meat from under her garment. She had brought it for her meal along with a seed cake. She moved a little closer to the wolf pup and held out the meat.

The pup raised the fur on its neck and growled feebly. When it caught the scent of the meat, it sniffed and sought the source of the smell. The pup drew nearer to Maddia and the meat. The pup snatched the meat from her, backed away, and began to chew it. From the way it took the meat, Maddia could tell that the pup had not eaten much meat before. She recalled that Lartha, the clan healer, had said that baby wolves drank their mother's milk just like humans. This pup had probably begun to eat meat only recently.

Reaching into her tunic again, Maddia removed a seed cake. She broke off a morsel and held it out to the pup. The young wolf peered at the meat and then the seed cake. It took the morsel of seed cake from Maddia, chewed it a few times, and then swallowed it. Because the seed cake was softer than the dried meat, the pup had an easier time eating it. The pup then continued gnawing on the dried meat.

Maddia withdrew from the cave carefully while watching the wolf pup, which was concentrating on the dried meat. She did not want to frighten or disturb the pup while it was eating.

Without saying a word, Maddia pulled another strip of dried meat from her brother's tunic, indicating with a nod that it was for the pup. Lakus, who was going to protest, finally understood. He allowed Maddia to take his meat but was confused when she appeared to eat it.

Maddia chewed the meat to soften it as she walked to the cave. The pup glanced at her, but returned quickly to the food it had. Maddia dropped the meat by the pup, who caught the scent of the meat and then seized it, eating this new treat more easily than the dried piece.

Once more, Maddia backed out of the cave. She led Lakus and Ganni a short distance away. She told them in hushed tones that she thought the pup had been abandoned. It was very hungry and terribly thin.

"We can kill the wolf and bring it to camp," said Lakus. "I can wear its skin."

Ganni frowned at the boy but replied sincerely, "There is no pride in killing a tiny pup, Lakus. Besides, as Baratho has told us, all creatures are our brothers and sisters. We should only kill if we need food or to keep ourselves from harm."

"You will have many chances to exhibit your bravery," said Maddia, touching her brother's arm. "Let us ask Lartha what we should do with the pup. For now, tell no others, not even our families."

The three of them hurried to camp, carrying the tool stones they had found. As they left, Maddia looked over her shoulder and saw the wolf pup gnawing the dried meat. It paused for a moment and gazed at her. For an instant, Maddia sensed something strange and wonderful, as if a secret were being passed between her and the wolf pup. It was a feeling she would remember for the rest of her life.

Chapter 3

Arriving at the camp, the children brought their rocks to Fong, the clan's toolmaker. He had joined the clan years ago because his own clan had been destroyed by a deadly sickness. His people had come from a distant land hoping to escape the sickness, but it had followed them. The individuals who had survived had been brought into new clans, usually as slaves. Fong was fortunate because Baratho had recognized his skills as a toolmaker. He was considered a valued member of the clan.

As they put their stones in the heap by Fong's shelter, they hoped that he did not notice that they had acquired fewer than usual. They underestimated him.

"You three are usually the best finders, yet today you have few stones. Did the wolves frighten you into returning to camp?" Fong raised his eyebrows as he spoke.

At the mention of wolves, the three children

took a quick breath. After a short and awkward silence, Maddia answered with an apologetic tone, "I was a little concerned, Fong. There were signs that wolves were around. Do not blame the boys. I just wanted us to be safe."

Fong looked at the girl suspiciously but good-naturedly. He knew she was fearless under most circumstances, but perhaps she was being protective of her younger brother. "You did the right thing, Maddia. It is better to be cautious when wolves are nearby. You will have plenty of chances to seek tool stones."

Saying farewell to Fong, the three children went to Lartha's shelter. It was a niche in a cliff that had been partially enclosed with logs, skins, and brush. Around the exterior of the shelter were remnants of bone, horn, and teeth from animals. They hung from trees and bushes or were arranged on the ground in strange patterns. The outside walls of the shelter and much of the interior were covered with pieces of plants that Lartha used to make brews for sicknesses, bad feelings, and other conditions that brought the members of the clan to her for help.

"You have something to tell me?" said a voice from inside the shelter.

Hearing Lartha's words before they had announced themselves startled the three children. Everyone in the clan wondered how Lartha gave the impression of being one step ahead of them, as if she existed in a different time.

"Good day, Lartha. May we come in? We have a

matter to discuss with you, but it is for your ears only," said Maddia quietly.

"Come in, children," invited Lartha. "What is it that can be shared with an old woman and not the clan?"

Anyone who entered Lartha's shelter was somewhat disoriented. The smell of drying plants filled the air, and all sorts of peculiar artifacts were scattered around the shelter. Some were dangling from the slanting walls, confusing visitors who had a difficult time adjusting to the mix of angled walls and hanging objects. Lartha had the habit of picking up interesting things and putting them in her shelter. In many cases, Lartha had no idea what she had acquired, but as time passed, she came up with an explanation that was meaningful to those who listened as well as to herself.

While studying the interior of the shelter, Maddia began to explain. "We found a wolf pup this morning while looking for tool rocks. There were no wolves to be seen, and it seemed as if none had been with the pup for days. I gave the pup dried meat and seed cake. It ate like it was starving, and I am worried about the pup. What should we do?"

Lartha, who was on the floor of her shelter, nodded as Maddia spoke. When Maddia had completed her description, Lartha asked the children to sit with her.

"For several nights, I have had a strange dream that I did not understand. In the dream, humans and wolves lived and traveled together, and the wolves were beloved by the humans. They journeyed to far places, and the humans built vast camps of stone and wood. Perhaps this wolf pup is part of my dream."

"Let me propose this," Lartha continued. "It is nature's way that the mother and the pack should care for the pup. Tomorrow the three of you can return. If there are signs of the mother or other wolves, then come back to camp, as you would normally do. Bring extra dried meat, and if the pup is still alone, feed it again. Spend time with the pup as you are gathering the tool rocks for Fong. Speak softly to one another and the pup. Maybe you can leave clothing you have worn in the front of the cave so the pup will have your scent with it. If the pup has been abandoned, taking these steps may help it become more trusting."

Maddia had been able to get as close as she had to the wolf pup for an unusual reason. For many generations, certain wolves were losing their fear of humans. In fact, two kinds of wolves had developed. The largest wolves were in packs that stayed far from humans and were fierce hunters. A smaller kind of wolf lived near human clans. These wolves hunted, but they were also willing to eat the meat that was unused after a human killed an animal.

Wolves and humans had coexisted for many thousands of years, and they had much in common. Wolves and humans sought the same prey, they were pack animals that preferred to be in groups, and they were capable of adapting to changing weather and climate. From the point of view of humans, however, there was an enormous problem: wolves sometimes hunted humans for food. It was rare when humans hunted wolves for food, but if there was a chance encounter, humans would try to kill the wolves to protect themselves.

Over time, the smaller type of wolf had learned that humans regularly left meat behind when they made a kill. This was particularly true with sizable animals like mammoths. Once the humans took all the meat they could carry, the wolves ate the remnants of the carcass.

In addition, humans disposed of uneaten food from their camp and put it in waste piles called middens a distance away. They knew that food in a camp attracted bears, lions, and wolves. Putting the uneaten food somewhere else was a way that humans could feel more secure. Wolves visited the middens where humans threw food scraps and ate what they could scavenge.

Some wolves did not do this and kept their distance from human settlements. The bolder wolves hunted and shared in the pack's kill, but they had an added supply of food. They were able to sustain themselves during hard times, and their pups had a better chance of living to maturity. Each generation of wolves became more familiar with humans. It is possible that Maddia's wolf pup had seen people wandering in the area. Because its mother did not show excessive fear, the wolf pup was less cautious of the animal that walked on two legs.

Chapter 4

The next day, the three of them did as Lartha had suggested. When they went to search for tool rocks, they brought extra food. Before going to the cave, they climbed up a ridge and looked carefully for wolves. They saw nothing to indicate that wolves had been there, but that was not enough assurance for Ganni.

"Let me walk to the trees," said Ganni. "I will look for wolves on the way. You two wait here and warn me if any come from afar."

Ganni made his way down the ridge and hurried across the field toward the forest. He looked around cautiously, turning often to see if Maddia or Lakus signaled danger. Reaching the trees, he inhaled the air through his nose, trying to catch the faintest trace of the characteristic smell of wolf. Feeling confident they were in no immediate danger, he waved to his cousins and started toward them.

Suddenly, Ganni came to a standstill. Another figure had stepped from the trees. It was Jartush, a member of the clan, but no friend of Ganni's family. Jartush was the brother of Gortush, and most who knew them despised both of the men.

"What are you doing here by yourself, boy?" Jartush called out harshly as he strode toward Ganni.

Maddia saw a man advance toward Ganni, but at such a distance, she could not distinguish who it was. More than likely, it was someone from their clan. She had no desire for anyone to learn of the wolf pup, so she tapped Lakus on the shoulder and motioned for him to be quiet and come with her. She climbed down from the ridge, being careful to avoid the cave. Maddia didn't want to agitate the wolf pup or give away its location to whoever was with Ganni.

The two of them ran toward Ganni, who glanced their way. Jartush followed Ganni's eyes and saw the two children.

"It is Maddia and Lakus," said Ganni. "We are collecting stones that Fong can use for tools. I was looking for any indication of wolves before beginning."

Ganni was respectful to Jartush, hiding his disdain for the brother of Gortush. He did not want a confrontation with Jartush in order to keep their real purpose a secret. It was not the clan's way for a young person to be impolite, even if the person was being as unpleasant as Jartush.

Jartush looked at Ganni. The boy was approaching manhood and had proven his strength and courage in many hunts with the men. Nonetheless, Jartush treated him badly. "Go with the other children and do your job." With that, Jartush turned and headed toward the camp. He paid no mind to Maddia and Lakus.

Although he felt intense anger at the insult, Ganni did not say anything and simply looked at the ground. *Some day,* he thought, *you will pay for the way you and your brother have treated us.*

"What was Jartush doing?" asked Maddia.

"I have no idea," answered Ganni. He gripped his staff tightly, and Maddia could see he was angry.

"He is a worm," commented Maddia, "as is his brother. I think he was up to no good."

They waited until Jartush was out of sight before returning to the cave. The boys stayed at a distance and began looking for the tool stones. Maddia edged silently to the opening.

The wolf pup greeted her with a growl, but it was not so fierce as yesterday. Maddia took meat and seed cakes from her tunic. She offered the pup some of each, and as it had done before, the wolf ate the food greedily.

After finishing the meat and seed cake, the pup slid a little nearer to Maddia. It did not growl but remained wary. Maddia spoke in a low voice to the pup and placed more food at an arm's length. To get the food, the pup had to crawl closer to Maddia.

The pup picked up a morsel of meat, but instead of going to the rear of the cave, it settled in next to Maddia and chewed the meat. When it had consumed the first piece, the pup ate the rest of the food deliberately, looking at Maddia as it did.

Allowing a short time to pass, Maddia backed away slowly from the cave. The wolf pup watched her but made no attempt to come with Maddia. It did not, however, crawl to the far end of the den.

The three cousins spent the morning looking for tool stones. Every once in a while, they looked toward the cave. The pup was usually watching them. One of these times, it came out of the den and drank water from the spring. When the sun was straight overhead, it was time to head back to camp. Before leaving the area, Maddia went back to the cave. She whispered to the pup, using the words and tone she had heard mothers use with babies. She gave the pup a little more food, and before she withdrew her hand, she held it out for a moment. The pup smelled her hand and licked it gently before eating the food she had left. Maddia was thrilled.

The next day was much the same. There were no signs of wolves, and when Maddia came to the den, the pup wagged its tail. As she fed the pup, it licked her hand fondly several times. To Maddia, it seemed as if the pup was no longer as afraid of her as it had been at first.

On the way to camp, Maddia said to the boys, "Let us confer again with Lartha. The pup has no family, and she is losing her fear of me."

"The pup is a girl?" asked Lakus.

"Yes," answered Maddia, "I saw she was a girl,

and her name is Nasha."

"That is the name of our sister who passed on," said Lakus. "Is it a fitting name?"

"I think so," said Maddia. "Nasha was the first-born child in our family. She passed to the next life after just a few days with mother and father. They are sad when they mention her. I think that hearing her name will make them feel better."

Reaching Lartha's shelter, the children were received warmly. The three of them chattered together, excitedly telling Lartha of the events of the past days. When Maddia mentioned to Lartha the name she had chosen for the wolf pup, the woman put her hand on Maddia's cheek. "You have chosen well. Your parents were deeply saddened by the passing of their child. The name you have selected will lessen their pain."

Lartha looked at Maddia and the boys, then she continued. "May I see this wolf pup for myself? Maddia can bring me to the pup so I can discover more about it. No one in the clan should be told of the pup yet. The three of you must be silent about it. Lakus and Ganni, you boys stay in camp and go about your chores as you would usually do. I will tell Zibio and Belia that Maddia is helping me collect medicine plants. Let us be on our way."

Leaning on her staff, Lartha got to her feet and picked up a piece of folded leather with meat inside. The three children rose also, and the four of them left the shelter.

"Remember, not a word of this to anyone,"

Lartha reminded the boys. "Come, let us speak with Zibio and Belia."

Lartha explained to Maddia's parents that the two of them were going to collect medicine plants. There was nothing strange about this because Lartha often requested assistance when she collected plants, and Maddia was her favorite companion. The girl was good company and had sharp eyes and a clever mind. Many in the clan thought that in the future, Maddia would be a healer.

Maddia led Lartha to the cave that was the pup's home. Before advancing too close, they looked around for the wolf pack and for other members of the clan. When they were sure there were no wolves or people in the vicinity, they slipped quietly to the small cave.

At first, it seemed as if the cave was empty and the pup was gone. Disappointed and a little sad, Maddia got down and looked more closely. In the shadows in the back of the cave, Maddia spotted the form of the sleeping pup. Without making a sound, Maddia pointed it out to Lartha, who shook her head with understanding.

The two of them retreated from the entrance to the cave. When they were far enough away so that their voices would not awaken the pup, Maddia asked, "What should we do?"

Pausing, Lartha looked around warily. "The wolves have not been here for days," she observed. "I do not know what prompted them to depart, but it is unusual for a mother wolf to abandon a pup no matter what. We cannot leave the pup to die."

Maddia nodded and a smile crept across her face. She was relieved that Lartha, who had great influence with the clan, felt the same way she did. She leaned forward and gave Lartha a hug.

"To my recollection, no one has ever brought a wolf pup to our clan or any other. I am uncertain about the best course of action." Lartha thought about the situation and then asked Maddia what she wanted to do.

Maddia replied so suddenly that she astonished even herself. "I will go into the cave with the pup. When she wakes up, maybe she will think I am her mother or another wolf."

Lartha was about to insist that would not happen, and then she stopped. *Why not?* she thought. *I have no better idea, and who is to say that is not the correct thing to do?* "Your suggestion is more suitable than any I have," said Lartha. "Let us try it."

They turned and walked to the cave. On the way, Lartha passed to Maddia some pieces of meat from the folded leather. "These are from my early meal today," she said. "They are soft from cooking. Perhaps the pup will be hungry when it awakens. As its new mother, you will be responsible for feeding the pup as well as protecting it."

Tiptoeing softly, the two of them approached the cave. Maddia could see that the pup was sleeping. She nodded at Lartha and lay down on her belly. Carefully and quietly, Maddia crept into the cave.

The pup did not awaken as she drew near. Its

breathing was slow and regular, meaning that it was asleep. Maddia was able to get beside the pup without disturbing it. She resisted the temptation to stroke the pup's fur, and instead, assumed a comfortable position. She looked over her shoulder at Lartha and winked.

Remaining still for a while, Maddia began to feel drowsy. She closed her eyes, laid her head on her arm, and dozed off to sleep. She was awakened shortly by a stirring against her chest. Looking down, she could see the sleepy pup poking its nose at the fur of her tunic. Maddia had no idea what to expect.

As it woke up, the pup continued to snuggle up to Maddia, who looked at Lartha crouched at the entry to the cave. The older woman did not say anything, but Lartha made a stroking motion with her hand. Maddia understood and petted the wolf pup, drawing it closer to her. The pup did not resist and uttered a sigh, enjoying the company of another living creature. It had been days since the mother had gone hunting with the pack, never to return, and the pup was lonely.

The pup settled farther into Maddia's tunic, but it was not yet fully awake. Maddia decided to take a chance. She clutched the pup to her tunic, rolled to her side, and slid toward the front of the cave. Lartha, understanding what the girl was doing, nodded in support.

Reaching the mouth of the cave, Maddia circled around and began to back out. She wanted to place her body between the pup and the light coming from the outside so it would not be startled. She could feel the pup shifting and knew it would soon wake up. Maddia sensed Lartha's hands under her arms pulling upward and making it easier for her to stand.

Once on her feet, Maddia was wobbly because of being down so long. In addition, the pup was now alert and squirming inside her tunic. Maddia tried to hold the pup so it would struggle less, but she was worried that she might hurt it.

As quickly as they started, the pup's movements ceased. Distressed, Maddia looked down and saw why. The pup had found a scrap of meat that was under her tunic. Maddia turned to Lartha so she could see what the pup was doing. The healer pointed in the direction of the camp, and the two of them walked home. On the way, Maddia experienced a special kind of joy she had not sensed before.

Neither spoke a word on the way to camp. They didn't want to disturb the pup, which was so busy chewing the meat that it didn't notice that it was being carried from the cave. When the pup had almost finished the meat, Maddia let it have an additional piece.

As they neared the camp, Lartha led Maddia to a rarely used path that skirted the main cluster of dwellings and brought them to Lartha's shelter. They were not ready to explain to the rest of the clan what they were doing with a wolf pup. They slipped into the shelter, and Lartha drew the hide that served as her door over the entryway.

Chapter 5

The interior of Lartha's shelter was dim. A little brightness came in through gaps in the wall. Maddia brought the pup to a corner and knelt down carefully. She placed Nasha beside her on some animal skins.

The tiny wolf stopped chewing the meat and looked at her surroundings. She sniffed the air, glanced at Lartha, and put her head on Maddia's lap. The pup sighed and fell asleep almost instantly.

Speaking quietly, Lartha said, "Your idea has worked. The pup thinks you are her mother." The healer looked thoughtfully at Maddia. "I cannot hazard a guess about how the people of the clan will take the news of a wolf pup living with us. Let us keep her a secret for the time being. The pup can stay here. You can care for her easily. Practically no one comes to my shelter, and you can take Nasha for walks between the shelter and the running water."

Lartha's shelter was at the edge of the camp

beside a stream. Part of the shelter was built into the side of a hill. A thick grove of trees and shrubs grew between the hill and the river. Maddia could take the pup outside without being seen by the other clan members.

With a sleepy yawn, Nasha woke from her brief nap. She licked Maddia's hand, stretched, and stood up. Maddia rose and took a few steps to leave the shelter. Nasha followed behind, examining with a puppy's curiosity the objects that Lartha had assembled. Maddia pushed aside the hide covering the opening and went through it.

Nasha did not, however, immediately follow Maddia into an unfamiliar area. She whimpered and trembled unsurely but did not proceed.

"Come, Nasha," whispered Maddia. The girl knelt on all fours near the shelter. Hesitantly, the pup took a few paces and then pranced more boldly. She went to Maddia and positioned herself in the protected space between the girl's arms and legs.

"Hold that position for a moment," said Lartha. "It is a more wolf-like pose than being upright. The pup will be more comfortable."

Nasha looked here and there. She nosed around thoroughly, but all the while keeping close to the girl. Maddia stroked the pup's back and tail. A short distance away, a grasshopper bounded off and landed. Immediately, Nasha dropped to the ground in the hunting position of a wolf. She crept stealthily from under Maddia's chest. When she was within

25

a few feet of the grasshopper, she pounced. The bug leaped out of reach before Nasha could trap it.

"Did you see that, Lartha?" asked Maddia. "How does she know what to do? It was as if she was born to hunt."

"That is exactly right. She was born to hunt," said Lartha. "Animal babies are different from us. They come into the world with an understanding of what they should do in many situations. We humans must be taught almost everything by our parents and our clan. You may be taken aback at the things that Nasha can do." Lartha was silent and then asked, "I wonder what she will learn from us, and what we will learn from her?"

The two of them looked at Nasha, who was chasing a leaf being blown by the wind. She would lunge at the leaf and lift her paw to see what she had caught. When she did, the breeze would sweep the leaf away again, and Nasha would persist in chasing it. She never got far from Maddia, however, and often looked in her direction to assure herself that the girl was still there.

Maddia stood up, and Lartha came out of her shelter. They walked for a short distance and waited while Nasha squatted in the bushes.

"I did not consider that," said Maddia. "Nasha realizes that she must relieve herself outside the shelter. That is good, is it not?"

"Yes, it is," answered Lartha, "but I am not optimistic she will be able to do it every time it is necessary. We shall see, but it is probably sensible for you to spend as much time as you can with her outdoors."

Nasha came to the edge of the stream. She studied the flowing water and touched it tentatively with her paw. She backed up and then returned to the water. She was curious but showed no sign of wanting to wade into the stream.

"I have not seen a wolf near the water," said Lartha, "Some animals swim, but I don't know if a wolf can. For now, it is better that she does not try to go in the water."

Hearing unexpected voices, Lartha and Maddia were alarmed. Lartha began at once to rush toward them. Maddia went to Nasha and scooped up the pup. She headed into the thicket of trees next to the stream. The pup fidgeted in her arms impatiently, wanting to continue exploring on the ground. Maddia's anxiety diminished when she recognized that the voices belonged to Lakus and Ganni.

"What did you decide about the wolf pup?" asked Ganni. Lartha said nothing but looked toward the trees. Maddia stepped from her hiding place. "I see," said Ganni, grinning. He was pleased when he noticed Maddia holding the pup.

"Give the pup all the time she needs to get used to you," suggested Lartha. "She has taken well to Maddia, but she otherwise has little experience with humans."

The boys nodded in agreement, and the three of them went to the shelter. Maddia put Nasha down and wandered toward Lartha's dwelling. The pup trailed behind, and on the way, picked up a small stick. She trotted proudly up to Maddia with the stick as if she were bearing a gift. Maddia bent down to accept it, but Nasha turned her head quickly and withdrew. She came back to Maddia, but each time the girl reached for the stick, the wolf dashed off.

Seeing what was happening, Lartha laughed and said, "The pup is playing with you. I have seen other wolves chasing one another with sticks. I think it helps young wolves become strong and bond with members of their pack."

For a while, Maddia and Nasha played the game. When Maddia grasped the stick, Nasha growled and pulled against her. It was clear the pup was having a wonderful time, but she was becoming tired. The pup ran a final circle around Maddia and came up to her panting. Nasha dropped the stick at Maddia's feet and lay down exhausted in front of her. Maddia picked Nasha up and brought her face close to the pup's nose. Nasha licked Maddia's chin as the girl walked toward the shelter. By the time they got to the hut, Nasha was fast asleep in Maddia's arms.

Maddia went inside, sat down on the animal skins in the corner, and put Nasha beside her. The two boys seated themselves on the other side of the hut.

"We have to tell your parents about Nasha," said Lartha.

"I know," sighed Maddia. "Do you think they will let me keep her? If they do not, what should I do? I cannot forsake her."

Lakus spoke confidently. "They will let you keep Nasha. She is our sister."

"Perhaps, but I cannot speak for your mother and father," said Lartha, "They are thoughtful and love you more than you will ever know. I think they will be fair to you, the wolf pup, and the clan. Let me go to your shelter and bring them here. I would like them to meet Nasha before they make a decision. Wait for me. The boys will stay with you."

"Can I touch her?" asked Ganni.

"Yes," answered Maddia, "and you, too, Lakus. Try not to wake her."

The two boys crawled noiselessly to the sleeping pup. Each of them petted her cautiously, astounded that they were touching a wolf.

"We will do whatever we can to keep her from harm," said Ganni. "There is something special about her. I can feel it."

The sound of footsteps coming their way signaled the arrival of Lartha, Zibio, and Belia. Lartha had not told them why she wanted them to come to her shelter, but she had requested that they be quiet. They came into the shelter wondering what to expect.

The three on the ground looked up at the adults. Lakus and Ganni shifted positions a little so the newcomers could see the sleeping Nasha.

For a moment, all were silent. Zibio and Belia looked with wonder at Maddia and the wolf pup.

"I cannot believe what I am seeing," said Belia.

"How is it possible for my daughter to capture a wolf pup?"

"The wolf pup has not been captured," answered Lartha. "She was abandoned by the pack, and Maddia saved her. Somehow, Maddia has enchanted the pup. She thinks Maddia is her mother."

"Will not the pup grow up to seek her pack? What will the wolves do?" Zibio had a worried look, but he was not angry. He was expressing real concerns about the safety of his family and the clan.

"Wake the pup, Maddia," advised Lartha. To Zibio and Belia she said, "See how the pup and Maddia get along."

Maddia stroked the wolf pup's back. Lazily, the pup awakened, stretched, and looked up at Maddia. With a sleepy yawn, the pup rolled over on her back so Maddia could scratch her belly. She did not take her eyes from the girl who now meant so much to her.

"We have new friends for you to meet," whispered Maddia, and she lifted the pup gently. Stroking the pup, Maddia put Nasha on her lap so she could look around.

Seeing the new humans, the pup let out a low, defensive growl, but she did not budge. Nasha sniffed and looked from one person to another. Maddia reached over and picked up a piece of dried meat. She chewed it briefly to soften it and presented it to the pup. As she ate, the pup ignored the humans in the hut.

"We encountered the pup by accident some

days ago while looking for tool stones," said Ganni. "Maddia fed her, and we asked Lartha what to do." It was clear that Ganni was trying to protect the pup and his cousin by assuming part of the responsibility for what happened.

"You should see her run," added Lakus. "She can chase sticks, too." Beaming, he said, "Ganni and I were able to pet her."

Zibio put his hand on Belia's shoulder and spoke to Maddia. "You want to keep the wolf pup. That is why we are here, is it not?"

No words came to Maddia. She stroked Nasha and looked at her parents. Truthfully, she did not know what to say to them, and she was worried that if she said anything, she would cry, or worse, make her mother cry.

Lartha broke the silence. "Yes, Maddia would like to keep the wolf pup. Her name is Nasha."

Zibio drew his wife closer when he heard the pup's name. "That is the name of the sister you did not know."

"Yes, that is why I chose the name," replied Maddia. "From the first time I saw Nasha, I was aware that we shared an unusual bond. It was as if she recognized me."

Hearing that, Belia surprised everyone by smiling. "Lartha has said that when we die, part of us lives on. She is uncertain where this part goes, but perhaps this unseen spirit of a person can visit the living in a mysterious way. It is a fitting name."

Belia patted the earth beside her and whispered,

31

"Come, Nasha." The pup rose from her lying position and went to Belia. She touched Belia and Zibio with her nose, walked in a circle, and plopped down between them.

"Yes," stated Zibio, "it is a very suitable name. You have done well, Maddia."

Chapter 6

The young people and Nasha passed the night with Lartha. They agreed that being with several humans overnight would encourage Nasha to become more comfortable with the new people she would eventually meet. Zibio and Belia went home, revealing nothing of the wolf pup to others in the camp. They felt that it was unwise to tell the clan about Nasha.

The next day, Lartha and the children remained by the shelter. They spent some time gathering plants for food and catching fish in the stream. Nasha stayed with them, behaving as if she were with her new pack. Maddia gave Nasha small pieces of meat once in a while so the pup would not wander off.

Although they presumed that no one had seen the wolf pup, they were wrong. From the top of a hill, two hidden figures observed Lartha, the children, and the pup.

"I thought it was odd when I saw Ganni near the forest. There was no reason for him to be there if they were indeed collecting tool stones," said Jartush.

"Look at the wolf pup," whispered Gortush angrily. "It plays with them as if it is another child. I hope it grows up to turn on them, or that its pack comes for them." He snarled, "They have put us all in danger. We must tell Baratho. He will make the child abandon the wolf pup."

Hurriedly, the two brothers returned to the center of camp and located the clan leader. They told Baratho what they saw and demanded a council. He had no choice but to call a meeting of the elders and confront Maddia.

Baratho told Zibio and Belia about the council and how he had been informed about the wolf pup. He told them to bring Maddia and the wolf pup to the central hut that was used for important meetings. Reluctantly, they did as they were ordered, knowing they had little choice in the matter. Both of them had a bad feeling regarding what would happen. They lingered outside the hut with the rest of the clan. Most of those who had come together had no idea what had happened, and they were amazed to see Maddia carry a wolf pup into the hut. In a surprisingly short while, word of the wolf pup spread throughout the clan.

The crowd outside the main hut grew with every passing minute. They had learned of Maddia and the wolf pup, and everyone wanted to see it, especially the children. They also wanted to hear what Baratho's decision was.

Maddia was bewildered to see that so many spectators had congregated. They waited silently but craned their necks to see the pup, which by now was becoming fidgety. Zibio and Belia were right beside the opening of the hut, as were Lakus and Ganni. Lartha accompanied Maddia and the pup.

"Baratho has decided that Maddia can keep the wolf pup," said Lartha.

Upon hearing her words, many of the bystanders gasped. Never in the history of the clan had a wolf been welcomed to join them. There was muttering and grumbling from one or two of them, but curiosity about the wolf pup quieted the unfavorable comments.

Dropping to her knees, Maddia placed Nasha on the ground. Curious, the pup looked around. Recognizing some of the humans, it bounded to Belia and Zibio, licking their hands as they petted her. Nasha then turned to Lakus, and seeing a loose fragment of leather on one of his foot coverings, started to tug at it. Ganni knelt down with Nasha and held a piece of meat near her. She stopped tugging at the leather and began chewing the meat instead.

The people of the clan could not believe what they were seeing. The wolf pup was acting like a human child! Maddia had, indeed, enchanted the pup.

After eating the meat, Nasha got up and strutted

over to Maddia, who picked her up. With Zibio and Belia, Maddia strolled toward their shelter. Ganni and Lakus trailed after them. As they made their way through the crowd, it separated, but many of the children stayed in the front so they could see the wolf pup better.

As they approached their home shelter, Maddia saw her aunt, Leeza, standing with Checo, the clan's poet. Checo had been blind from when he was a child and owed his life to his ability to tell elaborate tales and to the intercession of Lartha. In the time of the clans, life was difficult. Those who were weak, infirm, or injured did not usually live to maturity. It was a question of survival for the clan. Each person had to contribute to the good of the clan. Family members cared for one another as well as they could. If individuals could not travel with the clan and perform a meaningful role, they were left on their own.

"Checo, you undoubtedly have heard of the wolf pup. Do you want to pet her?" asked Maddia. "She is losing her fear of humans, but I am not sure how she will act."

"Yes, my child, I am aware of the story of the enchanted pup. It would please me to pet the wolf pup. I understand that she may be shy." Checo's voice was soft, for he recognized that a subdued tone would be less likely to frighten the pup. "Have you bestowed a name on her?"

"Her name is Nasha," responded Maddia, and she walked to Checo's side. She guided his hand to

Nasha's nose so she could sniff it. Nasha licked Checo's hand and then pushed her head into it, allowing him to stroke her ears.

"The wolf pup is brave and loving," whispered Checo. "The name you have chosen could not be more fitting. What is her color?"

Before answering, Maddia thought for a moment and looked at Nasha reflectively. "She is mostly gray, but there are lighter parts on her face near her eyes and mouth. Her belly is gray, too."

"May I touch her?" asked Leeza.

"Of course," answered Maddia. "You are her aunt, as you are mine. I think you will love the feel of her fur."

Leeza was Belia's sister, and she had been close to Maddia from the girl's birth. Leeza was clever with her hands and could make many useful things. She and Fong discovered how to use strips of animal hide to tie stones to sticks to make throwing and cutting tools that were superior to what the clan had before.

"Yes, her fur is comfortable to the touch," added Leeza. "Did you notice the color of her eyes? They are blue, similar to the color of the sky."

"Are Nasha's colors the same as those of other wolves?" asked Checo.

"Many wolves are gray, but some are white. A few are very dark, just about black," said Leeza. "The eyes of most adult wolves are brown, but one or two in each pack will have blue eyes. I am sorry, Checo. These colors mean nothing to you, do they not?"

"There is no need to be sorry," said Checo. "You have told me what you see. I must use my mind to enrich the feeling of my hands so I understand Nasha better. I suspect that in years to come, I will often be asked to tell of the wolf who became a friend of humans."

Nasha was restless, so Maddia put her on the ground. The pup eyed the crowd that had clustered around her, and they stared back at her. The wolf's tail wagged slowly at first and then more quickly. She pranced to one person and then the next, smelling each one briefly and then returning to Maddia. Nasha was familiarizing herself with the members of her new pack.

"Come, Maddia," said Zibio. "We should go home now." He and Belia walked toward their shelter. Maddia followed, urging Nasha to stay near her, which she did, straying only a short distance occasionally to examine another new person or to glance inside a shelter. For the pup, the experience was like a completely new world.

When they reached the family shelter, Tulio was waiting there. He was the oldest child and was almost a man. He hunted with the men, and he would soon find a wife and construct a shelter of his own.

"Well, little sister, the report I have heard is true. You have enchanted a wolf pup and named her for our sister who is gone. It seems as if there is nothing that is beyond you." Tulio hugged his sister and lifted her off the ground, as he often did.

When Tulio put his hands on Maddia, something

happened that made everyone laugh. Nasha growled and challenged Tulio, who towered above many of the people in the clan.

"The pup is brave and protective," Tulio laughed. He put Maddia down and backed away from the pup to show that he recognized her bravery. He sat on the ground and asked Maddia to sit beside him. He then whispered to her and had her call Nasha.

The pup came to Maddia on the side farthest from Tulio, who asked his sister to pick Nasha up. With Nasha in Maddia's lap, he put his arm around his sister and stroked her hair. "I have watched wolves in a pack, and there is an order among them, much like humans. They have leaders and families, and the young imitate older members of the pack. I want Nasha to understand that I am in her family." Patiently, Tulio alternated strokes to Maddia's hair with caresses on Nasha's back.

It was not long before Nasha was licking Tulio's hand, so he gently scooped her up and brought her to his lap. From a fold in his tunic, he pulled out a piece of meat and chewed it. Unlike Maddia, however, he did not hand the meat to the pup. Instead, he put it between his teeth and bent over the pup. To the astonishment of the humans, Nasha took the meat from his mouth and ate it.

In addition to being a good hunter, Tulio was fascinated by the animals and the plants in the forest. He studied wolves, thinking that the more he knew of them, the safer he and his hunting group would be. Tulio did this from afar, often climbing a tree and keeping downwind from the pack. He had seen wolf pups lick the face of an older wolf to be rewarded by a piece of partially eaten meat. It was the way that pups made the change from their mother's milk to eating meat and eventually hunting with the pack.

"We will have to teach her to become accustomed to fire," suggested Tulio.

"My son is wise," said Belia proudly. "I did not think of that. Has Nasha seen fire since she has been with you?"

"Not at all," answered Maddia. "The weather has been warm, so Lartha has not had a fire in her shelter. We have kept Nasha hidden from the rest of the clan, so she has not seen the cooking fires or the great fire."

Lartha had come with the family to their shelter and commented, "Nasha may not have seen fire in her life. Her early days were spent near the plain of tool stones, and there is no fire there. She has not experienced fire in her time with us. She may not have the deep fear of fire that the majority of animals have. Is your household fire going now?"

"It is burning low with scarcely any embers," responded Belia. "Should we increase it?"

"Maintain the fire, but do not let it get too big," said Lartha. "We should let her become familiar with fire at her own pace. Let us go inside. Maddia, you stay with Nasha. We will stand in front of the fire so she will not see it. The fire is small, but it might frighten her."

The others went into the shelter, and shortly after, Maddia entered with Nasha at her side. The pup perceived at once from the familiar smells that this was her new den. The scent of humans, especially Maddia, was everywhere. She paid no mind to the fire surrounded by a ring of rocks at the edge of the shelter. The tiny bit of smoke from the fire drifted up through a hole in the roof.

"For the next few days, you should take Nasha outside if the fire must be large. Keep her away from the great fire, and bring her here only when the cooking fire is not blazing. You can share your food with her when you return. She may lose the fear of fire she and other animals naturally have." Lartha looked at Zibio and Belia. "Does that seem prudent to you?"

"That is a fine idea," said Zibio. He smiled when he spoke because he was grateful that Lartha recognized his capacity as head of the family. She was an elder and perhaps the wisest person in the clan, yet she treated him with substantial respect. She did not simply tell him what to do, which was her right, but sought his counsel and let him make the decision.

"What should we do with Nasha?" asked Maddia looking at those with her in the shelter. "Does she not have to adopt the ways of our clan?"

"Of course she does," replied Belia. "Maybe we should treat her the way we would a very young child. She can be with you as you do your chores.

Let her get to know the children and adults. Be sure she is fed, has water, and is clean. Play with her, talk to her, and help her grow strong. Lakus, you should assist Maddia, as should Tulio and your cousins."

When she finished, Belia patted the floor and murmured Nasha's name. The pup stopped wandering around the shelter and came over. Belia picked her up and rose to her feet. "Maddia, come with me for a moment. This might be a good time to take Nasha for a walk."

Maddia looked at her mother with a new sense of admiration. Belia had clearly been giving considerable thought to how Nasha should be treated, and already she favored the pup. Maddia could discover much about raising Nasha from her mother.

Chapter 7

Nasha's first days in the camp were busy from morning until night. She went everywhere with Maddia as she did the work expected of children. She had plenty of support because most of the other children in the camp wanted to spend time with the wolf pup. Zibio urged Maddia to do things in the camp, fearing that taking Nasha into the wild might put her and Maddia in danger from hunting animals.

As Lartha had surmised, Nasha exhibited little fear of fire. The more time she was around the fires that were used for cooking, the less nervous she became. On cool evenings, Maddia's family left the fire burning brightly to heat the shelter. Nasha would enjoy the warmth of the fire and lay down by it, but when it was time to sleep, she invariably snuggled up beside Maddia.

The fire that the clan kept going after sunset was a different story. This fire was bright and noisy so it would drive dangerous animals away. Nasha was not very comfortable with this fire and would not go near it, a fact that was observed by Gortush. He had never accepted Baratho's decision to allow Maddia to keep the wolf pup.

When it became clear that Nasha was so attached to Maddia that she would not run off, the sisters Belia and Leeza led a group of youngsters to the stream to catch fish for dinner. Tulio and Ganni served as their guards in case any wild animals or unfriendly hunters came by.

Spotting a bird's nest from the previous year, Ganni removed it from the tree and studied it thoroughly. "Tulio, did you ever notice how deliberately these nests are made?" he asked his cousin.

"Some are," answered Tulio, "but some are not. The big water birds with the long beak throw twigs together carelessly. I don't know how it keeps the eggs in. The nest you have found is made particularly well. Look at how the tiny pieces of grass and twigs are intertwined. This bird was precise in its choice of materials and construction."

Seeing her son and nephew studying the nest, Leeza went to them. Like the boys, she admired its beauty and usefulness.

"I have tried to imitate a bird's nest with sticks but have not been successful. My nests fall apart if I use sticks. When I use grass, it is not strong enough to hold anything." Leeza felt frustrated that a bird was capable of making something that she could not.

A movement in the willow branches in front of them was an indication of the arrival of a wet and muddy Nasha. She shook herself dry next to the three of them, and seeing they were doing nothing interesting, returned to the stream where Maddia and some children were attempting to catch fish.

"Look at the path that Nasha made as she came from the stream," said Tulio. "The branches did not break, but just bent. Now they are springing back to how they were before."

Because it was still early in the season, the willow branches did not yet have regular leaves. Green buds were beginning to show on each twig. Leeza grasped a branch and flexed it with her hand. As Tulio had noted, it did not break. She was even able to bend the twig over itself in her hand to tie it into a knot.

"Ganni, do you have your cutting stone?" asked his mother. She took the razor-edged stone that Fong had created for him and cut a handful of willow branches. Handing the stone back to him, she said, "Would the two of you cut more of these? Choose the thin branches similar to this that bend easily. I think there may be a way for us to borrow the bird's technique."

While the two boys cut dozens of willow branches, Leeza looked at the bird's nest more closely. She noted how many of the blades of grass were twisted together in a random way that kept the nest from falling to pieces. She realized that she could not compete with what the bird had done because there were hundreds of blades of grass and small twigs tangled together. Leeza paid special attention to the bottom of the nest and tried to understand how it was attached to the sides and cradled the eggs securely.

Putting her hands together to duplicate the configuration of the nest, Leeza studied her fingers. She separated them and then intertwined them together. With a grin, she put four willow branches on the ground in one direction and four on top of them in the other direction. She wove a branch through the others in an alternating pattern that matched her fingers and repeated it several more times. The eight willow twigs remained together, with lengths of willow extending in all directions.

Excitedly, Leeza bent the willow branches up into the form of a nest. They gradually returned to their original form, but Leeza knew what to do. She took another slim willow twig and began to weave it in and out of the twigs she had arranged. It went through them all and held them together. She did this again and again, overlapping each willow twig and weaving it among the sticks that formed the nest-like shape.

The two boys ceased their cutting of the willow twigs and watched in amazement. Before their eyes Leeza was making an object that was similar to a bird's nest but was bigger and stronger. It was an article no human had seen before.

Ganni touched the collection of twigs gently, afraid that his hand might cause it to disintegrate. He was surprised to feel how strong it was. His mother handed it to him, and Ganni turned it over in his hands. Without saying a word, he passed it on to Tulio.

"I have not ever seen anything of this kind, Leeza," uttered Tulio. As had Ganni, he felt the strength of the nest of willow. "No bird has ever made a nest so quickly or so strong."

"Here, let me have that," said Leeza with mock impatience. "Give me your cutting stone. I cannot have my nest be less beautiful than that of a bird."

With the sharpened stone, Leeza cut the odd twigs that stuck out. She adjusted the willow twigs to her satisfaction and pressed the sides of the creation to make it more round. Content with what she had made, she rose to join those who were catching fish, motioning for the boys to come along. Tulio carried the willow nest.

Running ahead of Leeza and Tulio, Ganni shouted with a justified sense of pride, "Look what my mother has made." His excitement drew the children and grown-ups near, and Nasha followed behind.

"It is a delightful nest," exclaimed Belia, "and better than that of any bird. I think there is much we might do with such a nest. Was it difficult to make?"

"Not very," replied Leeza. "I will show you how, sister."

"Here is something we can do," said Lakus. Before anyone could halt him, the impulsive boy snatched the willow nest and sprinted toward the stream. The fish they had caught swam in a tiny pool made of a circle of rocks in the water at the edge of the stream. The clan used this method to keep the fish alive and fresh until it was time to take them to the camp. Lakus grabbed each fish and threw it flopping into the willow nest. He then bounded back proudly to rejoin the group.

"That is a dreadful thing to do with Leeza's handiwork," said Belia to her son. She was stern, but her voice contained a hint of amusement.

"There is nothing wrong with what Lakus has done," said Leeza. "Just as birds use a nest for their eggs, this nest was made to hold things. None of us is inclined to carry fish to camp, so Lakus has made our day better. Come, let us bring the fish back for the evening meal."

At the camp, the fish were gutted and cooked on sticks held close to the great fire. Everyone admired Leeza's willow nest, most notably Checo, who turned it over and over in his hands, exclaiming how wonderful it felt and how practical it was. Ganni made everyone laugh by telling how Lakus had put the brilliant invention to such a lowly use.

After enjoying the fish and seed cakes, the clan converged around the fire. Leeza took her basket to the edge of the camp and hung it from the branch of a tree, hoping the night air would diminish the stink of fish from the willow. Knowing how Nasha was still wary of the great fire, Maddia sat a little farther away in the back of the group.

Baratho encouraged Leeza to explain how she

had made the willow nest. With exceptional thoroughness, she described how the nests of birds had puzzled her for years, but she had identified no suitable material to imitate them. Seeing Nasha bend the willow twigs prompted the idea for the material, and the nest that Tulio found had been her model.

"Checo, you have heard Leeza's story and handled the nest she has made. Do you have a name for this clever invention?" asked Baratho. He was confident that Checo would come up with a suitable name.

"You insist on testing my abilities, Baratho," said Checo with false gravity. Smiling, he continued, "As our esteemed leader, you demand much of us. It is no easy task to contrive a name for the splendid thing that Leeza has made. There are hardly any people who are as able with their hands as she is, although one could argue that Fong may be her equal."

Checo was often asked by Baratho, without any notice, to think of witty things to say or tales to tell. Checo typically responded by praising others, even if it was not completely sincere, which diverted the focus from the duty that was imposed upon him. In addition, his praise of those around him gave the poet time to think of a suitable response.

"Fong told me that the clan of his birth had another name for the nest of a bird. The word was *basket*. Perhaps we can borrow this name. Does that meet with your approval, Fong?"

Fong turned to Checo and answered pleasantly, "My old friend, you honor me by remembering what I told you long ago. I would be pleased if you would use a name from my former clan's tongue."

While the group was discussing the name that Checo had chosen, Maddia was trying to soothe Nasha. Initially, Maddia thought that she was reacting to the great fire. But the wolf pup was not looking at the fire; she was gazing intently toward the thicket of trees beyond the camp. Her whimpers turned to a low growl, and in an instant, Nasha sprang up and started barking loudly, walking toward the trees and then back to Maddia two or three times.

Zibio was becoming annoyed with Maddia and the pup, embarrassed that they had changed the tone of such an exceptional evening. Then he recognized that the pup was warning them. He jumped to his feet, as did Tulio. They picked up weapon stones and ran in the direction that Nasha was looking. More men joined them, but there was nothing to be seen. They were turning around when Leeza clasped her hands together and spoke in a broken voice.

"The basket is gone."

Chapter 8

"We can do no more tonight," stated Baratho. "The sky is dark, and there are too many dangers for us to go in pursuit. We will wait until tomorrow to seek whoever stole the basket." His tone sounded tired and disappointed. Others were equally dismayed, feeling that the disappearance of Leeza's basket was a terrible thing.

Leeza, however, immediately overcame her initial shock and gave the impression that she felt no sense of loss. An unusual look appeared on her face, and she addressed those around her peacefully. "Whoever took the basket is a fool as well as a thief. It has trivial value itself and stinks of fish. Tomorrow, I shall make another, and I shall teach each of you how to make baskets for yourselves."

On the following day, she did just that. Not a single person was concerned about the theft of the basket, but Nasha seemed to have identified the scent trail of whoever it was. Instead, the women

51

went down to the stream after the morning meal and collected willow twigs. They returned to the center of camp, and every woman, man, and child who was able learned how to make a basket. Checo, despite his blindness, made a fine basket, much to the amazement of those who saw him work deftly with his fingers.

As the clan members worked, Baratho scanned their faces. The only adults who were not engaged in the undertaking were the brothers Gortush and Jartush. The two brothers were frequently absent from the camp for days at a time, but where they went was a mystery. When they inevitably reappeared, they were unwilling to participate in the hunting, and a surprising number of people wished they would stay away. The brothers were eager to consume the food that was procured by those who were more ambitious, but they usually did as little as possible to obtain it.

Seeing Baratho glance from face to face, Fong commented, "You have noticed the brothers are missing, yet you do not judge them. You are a patient man, Baratho."

"I have been wrong regarding many things in the past," said Baratho. "I am reluctant to make an accusation that may be unfair at this time. Besides, this is a rare moment of joy for the clan. Not since we left our first home has everyone been this happy."

The clan did not always reside here on the fringe of the mountains where life was hard. In the past, they had a village close to an endless sea. The weather was better, friendly clans were nearby, and there was abundant food from the sea. They had been forced from their former lands by the neighboring clans because of Jartush and Gortush.

The brothers came from an old and respected family in the clan. Their father had been the head of the clan for a time, as had other ancestors. The brothers, in contrast, had been difficult from the beginning of their lives. When they reached manhood, they became no more tolerable. They took more than their share of food, were quick to anger, and had scant regard for anyone else.

On an afternoon long ago, the brothers saw two hunters from another clan kill a huge boar. It was too heavy for them to carry, so one of the hunters walked to his encampment to recruit help. Seeing an opportunity to be praised for their hunting skills, the brothers decided to drive the hunter away and claim the boar as their own.

The brothers' cruel nature was rivaled by their stupidity. Once they had driven off the hunter, they discovered that they, too, were unable to move the boar. The best they could do was to hack large pieces of meat from the boar, bring them to the village, and brag about the size of the animal they had killed.

Not long after the brothers arrived at the village, the hunters who had actually killed the boar showed up. With them were a host of men from the neighboring clans. Several hunting parties had observed the brothers' thoughtless actions, and the elders in each group had agreed upon a harsh punishment to be inflicted collectively on the clan. The brothers had broken the bond of fairness and cooperation that had allowed the clans to exist together in peace for many generations. Not only the brothers but the whole clan would have to leave the region. If they did not agree to exile, there would be a battle, and the clan of the brothers had no chance of winning a conflict against a coalition of the neighboring clans.

The chief of the clan at the time was Ushga, the father of Gortush and Jartush. Despite being shamed by his sons, he functioned as a wise leader. The next years were difficult, with the clan wandering from place to place in every season. Eventually, he brought them to the valleys in the foothills of the mountains. They probably could not stay here forever, for they must go where there was food, but they would survive in this location for a time. He made sure the clan was settled and appointed Baratho his successor, requesting that his sons remain part of the clan. Ushga then left the camp, never to be seen or heard from again.

The brothers caused no more serious trouble for the clan, but they were not on good terms with those who knew them. In recent years, the brothers had become obsessed with golden stones. No member of Baratho's clan had seen them, but travelers described the stones as if they truly existed.

The golden stones were different from typical

stones in many ways. Their gold color could be made to shine by rubbing, they became very soft—seeming to flow like water—when they were exposed to fire, and they could be shaped by striking them with other stones. Despite having no real value as tools or for any practical use, the golden stones were prized by some clans.

Because the golden stones were rare, the sole way for most people to obtain them was through trade. Few humans had anything of value that could be traded for golden stones, and the majority of them simply had no interest in stones that could not be made into tools.

For whatever reason, the sons of Ushga could think of little except the golden stones. Perhaps they thought that having the golden stones would bring them the esteem they had not earned. On the day that Ganni had encountered Jartush on the plain of tool stones, he had been trying to bargain with a trader from another clan for one of the stones, but he had been unsuccessful.

Seeing Leeza's nest of willow, the brothers understood at once that it could be traded for golden stones. All they had to do was figure out how to get it. When Leeza hung the basket at the edge of camp, the brothers knew they could steal it. Had the wolf pup not growled, they might have succeeded without raising the suspicion of Baratho or anyone else.

The brothers did not make their way far from camp. They carried the basket to the forest where Maddia had first encountered Nasha. They spent the night in a tree, which kept them safe from most of the hunting animals in the area. At dawn they proceeded on to a spot by the broad river where golden stones were sometimes discovered. They believed their basket could be traded for the stones that had driven them to such deceit.

While Jartush and Gortush were absent, the camp had been transformed. Baskets of all different sizes had been made, and within days, countless uses had been discovered for them. The members of the clan were pleased that they were able to make something, and for many of them, a basket was the first thing they had owned except their clothes. Fong put his finished tools and rough tool stones in separate baskets. When women and children went into the fields and forests for food, they returned with more than ever before because it was easier to carry things in a basket. Dried meat was put in baskets that were lodged in tree limbs to keep it from marauding animals. Such a substantial amount of food had been accumulated that there was even talk of possibly saving enough to maintain themselves in this camp through the winter.

Living in a permanent settlement was the dream of the clan. After their unfortunate exodus from their ancestral home, the clan had been forced to relocate at least two times a year. They yearned for their old ways with more substantial shelters and a dependable supply of food. Being a nomadic tribe was hard, and while wandering, it was sadly the case that some of the oldest and youngest died.

The place where they were living for this season was not as comfortable as their seaside home, but it did not have harsh winters, and the valley offered a certain level of sanctuary from dangers.

"Mother, do you really think that we might remain here through the winter?" asked Maddia. She stroked Nasha, who was lying with her.

"I do not know if the area can provide enough food for our needs, but it would be wonderful if we could settle here," said Belia wistfully. "You were not familiar with our existence in the village by the sea, but it was pleasant, and our shelters were bigger and more comfortable. I am optimistic that we can stay, at least for the next winter."

With Nasha at her side, and dreaming of a life without roaming, Maddia felt as peaceful as she had ever been. Her satisfaction soon dissipated, for in the distance she heard a pack of wolves howling. It was the first time she had heard the wolf song since finding Nasha, and she had no idea what Nasha would do.

The wolf pup was listening to the howling, also. Her ears perked up, and she sniffed the air several times. Nasha rose, inched her way to the opening of the shelter, and stared outside. She made muted whimpering sounds and then looked at Maddia and her mother.

It was a painful moment that Maddia knew would come, as did Belia. They did not speak, but they shared a sense of hope tinged with a fear of impending sadness. Nasha circled twice, looked out into the darkness briefly, and then walked to Maddia. She licked Maddia's hand and snuggled her head into the girl's chest. Humans were now Nasha's pack, and she was bound with them for always.

Chapter 9

Over the next days, the clan's routine slowly returned to its normal flow. A few of the women and children continued to make baskets, but most of them took up their everyday chores, and the men began hunting again.

Nasha had been with the clan for a relatively short period of time, but she had grown quickly. Her legs were longer, and she was not as skinny as when Maddia had found her. On the foraging trips with the women, Nasha neither lagged behind nor had to be carried. She also adopted a more protective role, being more aware of what was going on around her.

On a particularly fine day, Maddia and Nasha were in the earliest group of gatherers to depart from the camp. The mist was still in the air, and there was no noticeable wind. They drifted quietly through the forest to where mushrooms grew. The spring was the best time to search for this tasty food that was often wrapped in leaves and cooked with meat and vegetables.

In a clearing not far ahead, rabbits nibbled grass, paying little heed to the humans walking nearby. Noticing the rabbits, Nasha assumed a low crouch. Observing what she was doing, Maddia and the others came to a stop and watched her. Maddia smiled, remembering Nasha's failed attempt to catch the grasshopper. Nasha crept toward the rabbits, pausing when they glanced her way. The wolf's movements were imperceptible, yet she drew closer to the rabbits. Suddenly, she took off after the rabbits, hurtling at a speed that caught those who saw her off guard. In an instant, she had captured one of the rabbits by the neck, shook its head violently, and killed it. Nasha relaxed for a few seconds and then studied her kill. Rising from the ground, she grasped the rabbit in her jaws, pranced to Maddia, and dropped it at her feet.

Stunned at the swiftness of the attack and its success, Maddia could not believe what she had seen. Falling to her knees, she hugged the wolf and whispered, "Thank you, Nasha, for bringing us dinner. You are a skillful hunter."

Picking up the rabbit, Maddia handed it to her mother, who set about dressing the rabbit with a sharpened stone. Belia slit the rabbit's belly and removed the innards. She put fresh grass and herbs inside the carcass and tied the rabbit to her belt with a piece of leather. It was an unforeseen bounty that would be part of the evening meal.

While Belia dressed the rabbit, Maddia caressed Nasha and gave her hunks of dried meat and seed cake. She believed that the affection and treats would help Nasha understand that what she did was a good thing. The wagging of her tail made it apparent that Nasha delighted in both the treats and the attention she was receiving.

"Did you have any idea that Nasha was ready to hunt?" Maddia asked her mother.

"I had no idea," replied Belia. "A child of the same age cannot even eat without help. There are things we do not understand about wolves, and Nasha can increase our understanding of them."

The afternoon arrived, and the women went back to the camp in a cheerful mood. The day's activities had been successful. The baskets they had made allowed them to harvest more mushrooms and food plants than before, and Nasha had caught a rabbit. Maddia's family would eat well that night.

Late in the day, Gortush and Jartush returned to the camp. Although there was no way to be positive that they had stolen the basket, everyone suspected that they had. Not only were they gone from the camp when Leeza's basket was taken, but they proudly displayed some golden stones.

"So the golden stones do exist," commented Fong when the brothers showed them to him. "And they do shine like the sun. I wonder if the other legends about them are true?"

Fong's interest was as a toolmaker, and he exhibited to the brothers none of the deference they

61

expected the stones would bring. Nor did any of the clan members who were present. They did, however, have enormous regard for Leeza, whose invention of the basket and willingness to share it with the clan had enhanced their lives in a matter of days.

Fong persuaded the brothers to let him test the golden stones to see if the legends were accurate. The brothers consented because they anticipated that the toolmaker's endorsement might contribute to their status in the clan.

Putting one of the golden stones on his shaping rock, Fong tapped it with his hardest chipping stone. The golden stone's structure was altered just a little. With a few more taps and turns, he made the stone almost round, much to the entertainment of Gortush and Jartush.

The brothers were not pleased to hear Fong's next proposal. He wanted to put another golden stone in the fire. They feared it might burn up or lose its magic, but Fong's words were persuasive.

"Here is what I am thinking," argued Fong. "I shall put the golden stone on this holding stone." He pointed to a rock in which an indentation had been chipped. The rock held stones in place while Fong fashioned tools from them with a chipping stone. "If the golden stone does change as ice becomes water, it will not escape."

By now, Baratho and several men had congregated beside Fong's workplace. The brothers believed their importance had grown and agreed to the experiment that Fong had proposed.

Cautiously, Fong put a golden stone beside the fire. He chose a small stone with an odd shape. Nothing seemed to happen so he moved it closer to the fire. Again, nothing happened.

"The final element of the legend might be nothing but myth," suggested Baratho. "Perhaps the golden stones are not as magical as they are supposed to be."

Angrily, Jartush responded, "We have been cheated. These must not be golden stones."

"Let me think about this," said Fong. Staring at the fire briefly, he remarked, "I could not actually get the golden stone into the hottest part of the fire." His curiosity had been triggered by something his companions had not yet noticed. A tiny corner of the oddly shaped stone appeared to have changed slightly.

Fong put some rocks around and on top of the golden stone. He slipped the golden stone into the fire and pulled burning coals on top of it. Fong deposited more wood on the fire, and with a long, hollow reed, blew air into the fire. He had perfected this technique years ago as a way to make a fire when the wood was damp. Blowing on the fire made it grow brighter and hotter.

The fire blazed brightly, and Fong used a stick to arrange the hottest coals by the golden stone. The crowd that surrounded him was becoming restless, particularly the two brothers. Fong begged them to be patient and continued to blow into the fire, which had gotten so hot that the onlookers began to withdraw farther from it.

As the heat intensified, the toolmaker asked the brothers how they had obtained the stones. His question was intended to distract the bystanders and give the fire more time to work, but it produced a surprising result. The brothers were able to tell with whom they traded with and where the exchange happened, but not what they traded for the stones.

While the brothers stammered through their uncomfortable explanation, Fong made the fire blaze even hotter. When he thought the time was right, Fong cleared the embers from the stones. He then pushed the holding stone out of the fire and carefully tumbled the rest of the stones away. All of those who had converged on Fong's workspace were silent and tried to catch a glimpse of the golden stone. To their amazement, it had become a kind of liquid.

Fong struck the holding stone lightly and watched the melted gold stone jiggle in a way that was comparable to what water would have done. The liquid form did not last, and in a very short time, the stone became solid. The original shape of the golden stone was lost, and in its place was a flat slab with a gold color.

"What have you done with our golden stone," shouted Jartush anxiously, and he reached down to grab what was on the holding stone. He screamed in pain and dropped it at once because the golden stone was too hot to touch. Gortush, being just as greedy and no smarter than his brother, did exactly the same thing with an identical result.

"Your golden stone has not been damaged," said Fong, "it has merely been modified." His disdainful tone implied that he might have enjoyed the brothers' reckless attempt to handle the melted stone.

Fong slid the now-flattened golden stone onto a thick piece of animal skin. He picked it up and examined it closely. One side of the melted stone was as flat as ice on a pond. The other side matched the indentation in the holding stone.

Smiling broadly, Jartush pointed at the stone that Fong held. "The golden stones are truly magical," he said, "and their worth is unimaginable. My brother and I were wise to trade for them."

"I suppose they are as magical as water and ice," said Fong. "On a cold night in winter, the identical thing happens if water has pooled in the holding stone. It returns to water in the warmth of the sun the next day."

"I have observed this with ice at the edge of a stream," remarked Tulio, who had watched Fong's test of the stones. "The surface of the ice is flat, but the underside matches the bottom of the stream. You can even see the bumps caused by pebbles in the streambed. The golden stones are not magical, but they are different from more common stones, as Fong has shown. Perhaps one day in the future we will conceive of a use for a stone of this kind—as we found uses for the basket."

The pause that Tulio made when he spoke to

the brothers was not lost on those who surrounded Fong. His words were not a direct accusation, but they expressed the common belief that the brothers were in some way connected with the disappearance of Leeza's basket.

Hoping the melted golden stone had cooled enough to touch, Gortush snatched it from the piece of hide in which Fong held it. He and Jartush stormed away muttering about the mindless kinsmen who surrounded them.

Most of the group wandered back to their chores or family, but Tulio stayed to speak with Fong. "What do you think of the golden stones? Might they have real value?"

Fong answered thoughtfully. "That is a question I have asked myself, Tulio. I have no specific ideas yet, but I believe that there is much that can be done with the golden stones. People may be charmed by the beauty of the stones and their scarcity, but they may have worth we have not yet uncovered."

"Do you think there are additional kinds of stones that are like the golden stones?" asked Tulio. "Many things in nature are similar. Foxes and wolves are alike, and many of the seeds and fruit we eat are almost identical though they come from different plants. Might there be other things akin to the golden stones that are more plentiful and useful?"

"You have raised an important possibility," said Fong. "It would be marvelous if such stones were discovered."

Chapter 10

Spring turned to summer, and the days got warmer. Nasha had matured quickly, and her downy fur was stiffer and darker. Her eyes were no longer blue, but had become a golden brown. She looked more and more like an adult wolf, although she still had many of the traits of a pup.

One balmy afternoon, many of the women and youngsters were visiting a part of the stream that was special to the clan. A rockslide had blocked the flow of the stream, and a pool had formed behind the pile of rocks. Because the current was slowed, the pool was an excellent place to bathe. A second pool was below the rockslide, and this smaller pool had more fish than much of the stream because the fish could not swim upstream beyond the natural barrier formed by the rocks.

Maddia and her best friend, Katia, were wading in the upper pool. They were responsible for keeping the children close to shore where they would be safe. While humans had seen some animals swim, they were not able to swim themselves, and they were afraid of deep water.

The clan's fearfulness of deep water was partly the result of living by the sea for many years. Unlike this stream, the vast sea had waves and currents. It was not unusual for a human, most tragically a child, to be swept away, and death was inevitable.

Nasha was wandering along the bank a few paces from Maddia and Katia. Some of the boys and girls were with her, petting the wolf fearlessly. The children had known Nasha from her earliest days with the clan, and none of them had ever seen wolves in the wild or knew how dangerous they could be. To them, Nasha was a companion who was as harmless as another child.

At the far end of the pool grew a large tree with limbs that stretched in every direction. Evalen and her little brother, Noelo, were playing in the lower branches. The children of the clan were good climbers, so none of the women were uneasy.

While Evalen studied the flowers that were beginning to develop on the tree, Noelo scrambled higher. He was an adventurous boy who was constantly exploring, and he had little concern for his own well-being. In no time at all, he had climbed up the tree and was crawling on a sturdy branch that hung over the pool. He stood shakily on the branch and turned to boast to his sister about what he had done. As he attempted to turn, his foot snagged on a broken twig and he fell from the branch into the water.

Hearing the splash and then seeing her brother struggling in the water, Evalen screamed for help. Maddia hurried to shore and ran toward Evalen, with several of the women joining her. Nasha, seeing the women run together, acted instinctively and followed them.

Noelo continued thrashing in the water and began choking. Maddia and Belia waded into the water, but a sharp drop-off kept them from reaching Noelo. Evalen and the boy's mother, Murra, paced on the shore shouting his name.

Nasha was not sure what was going on and looked from person to person. Seeing Maddia and Belia in the water, Nasha went to them. She walked as far as she could and then paddled using the movements that come naturally to wolves. She swam to Maddia, who was standing in chest-deep water and could not understand how Nasha had gotten to her. The pup circled her and Belia playfully.

Spotting Noelo farther out in the pool, Nasha turned and paddled toward him, thinking that this was nothing but a game. By the time Nasha was with the boy, he was exhausted and slipped under the surface of the water. Nasha mischievously gripped the boy's tunic in her mouth and turned toward the shore. To the wolf pup, this was no different than chasing a stick and bringing it to Maddia.

As soon as Nasha got close enough, Maddia grabbed Noelo and pulled his head above the surface. Belia, being stronger, picked up the boy and trudged toward shore. Although he was choking,

Noelo was breathing.

Noelo had stopped coughing on the way to the shore. He gasped for breath, but it seemed he would be fine. His mother took him from Belia, thanking her profusely for saving her child.

"It was not I who saved Noelo," said Belia, "it was Nasha." She looked beside her at the wolf pup that was being hugged by Maddia. Nasha's tail wagged rapidly, but she broke from Maddia, took a step away, and shook the water from her coat. Everyone who was nearby was soaked, but there were no complaints, only laughter.

When the excitement died down, many of the mothers returned to the camp with their children. Maddia, Katia, and Tulio stayed behind. The day was too nice to be wasted, and the pool was among their favorite places.

"How was Nasha able to swim? She has not been taught, yet she swam with considerable skill. A similar thing happened when she saw the rabbit and was able to catch it." Maddia looked at Tulio, who probably had more understanding of plants and animals than any other clan member.

"I think you can answer your own question, sister. Animals are born with particular kinds of knowledge. No one demonstrates to birds how to build nests, yet they do. I have seen wolves cross streams and rivers by swimming, including pups no older than Nasha. Swimming might be in their nature, as are hunting and howling."

"Could we learn to swim?" asked Katia.

"It may be possible," responded Tulio. "We are like wolves in many ways. We live in packs, we eat meat when we can get it, and we hunt together. Perhaps we can learn to swim. Leeza learned to make baskets from examining the nests of birds. Of course, there is no risk in making baskets, but there is significant danger going in water that is deep. In the old days, many of our clan perished in the sea."

"But this is different," argued Katia. "I have never seen the sea, but my parents tell of huge waves. There are no waves here." She looked at Tulio and insisted, "I want to try to swim as Nasha does. Would you watch over me and keep me from going under the water if I fail?"

Tulio hesitated before answering. "It is a dangerous thing you want to do. If anything happened to you, I think your family would be very angry with me."

Maddia agreed with Tulio, but she had an idea. "Both of us can assist Katia. You are tall, so you can be in the deeper water. Nasha can swim to me to show Katia what to do. I think we can protect Katia."

Reluctantly, Tulio assented to Maddia's plan. He was troubled by the possibility that if he did not agree, Katia might try to swim when no others were around.

With his staff in his hand, Tulio strode into the pool until the water was up to his chest. Maddia accompanied him, but only to where the water was at the level of her waist. Nasha splashed happily beside her until the water was too deep for her legs. Then she started paddling.

Katia watched Nasha closely. She saw how the wolf kept her head above the water and paddled with her front and back paws. She did not stroke quickly but took her time. Katia walked to Maddia and leaned forward. Her feet were on the bottom of the stream, but she moved her hands as Nasha had moved her paws. Certain that she understood how to paddle, she leaned farther until her feet were no longer touching the streambed.

As the water crept up her neck and to her mouth and nose, Katia had a moment of alarm. She overcame her fear, continued paddling, and her head rose above the surface of the water. With a steady rhythm, she began to make progress. Nasha joined her, and the two of them glided through the water together.

Katia turned toward Tulio and went farther into the pool. She paddled by him before turning around and drifting toward Maddia. Nasha was with her the whole time. When the girl got into shallow water, she stood up and said breathlessly, "You should try it, Maddia! Swimming in water is unlike anything I have ever done before. I do not have words to describe the sensation, but it may be the same as birds feel when they fly."

"Try it, sister," said Tulio. "I will be right here. You will do fine."

Tulio's words and Katia's urging gave Maddia the confidence to try swimming. She slogged into moderately deeper water with Nasha, who was by now paddling. Maddia watched the pup and remembered what Katia had done. Taking a breath, she leaned into the water and moved her arms and legs as her friend had.

Maddia felt an intense sense of panic as the water crept past her chin. She shut her eyes and sputtered when the water reached her nose, but she kept paddling, determined to succeed. Her head stayed above the water, and she advanced forward as had Katia. With a broad smile, she paddled in a circle until she faced her friend.

"You were right, Katia. The feeling is wonderful." Maddia turned toward her brother and went out farther. "You must try it, Tulio."

Katia paddled confidently to Maddia and Nasha. The three of them played in the water joyfully, paddling in circles. The girls began to tire, so they swam toward the shore and reached water where they could stand up.

"Tulio, it is your turn. Katia and I will be ready to assist you if you need it."

The two girls were perplexed by what Tulio did next. Instead of coming into shallow water as they had done, he let his staff float and paddled from where he was. His head did not slip below the water, and he seemed to take to swimming much more readily than they had. They looked at him and wondered how he did it.

"I had the benefit of watching both of you as well as Nasha," insisted Tulio, seeing the look on their faces. "Your example helped me learn a little faster than you did, but the two of you were brave to try it first."

With apparently effortless strokes, Tulio swam to the girls and Nasha. He got on his feet and retrieved his staff, which had floated toward shore. "Let us rest and then swim some more," advised Tulio. "It is easy to forget things if they are not practiced. Besides, swimming is enjoyable."

Not wanting to have his staff in the way of their swimming, Tulio threw it toward the bank of the stream. Normally, he would have tossed the staff with two hands and set it spinning through the air. Because the girls and Nasha were with him, he did not want to risk injuring any of them. He held the staff over his shoulder, turned to the side, and threw it with one hand. He surprised himself at how far the staff flew and how straight it went.

"I have not seen you throw your staff in that way before," stated Maddia. "You do it well. You will have to explain to me how to do it."

After another swim, the three of them and Nasha returned to the camp. They considered sharing their ability to swim with their friends, but decided to put it off and practice another time. They wanted to be capable enough to instruct the others correctly.

On the way, Tulio threw his staff several times as he had in the pool. He continued to be impressed at how well it flew. He could not wait to reveal the technique to Zibio, and he wondered if he was the only person in the clan who knew of this method.

Chapter 11

Fong did not expect to see Tulio so late in the afternoon. "Should you not be having a meal with your family?" he asked the young man.

"I told my mother that I would be back in a while. She promised to set aside food for me, but between Lakus and Nasha, there might not be anything left. May I show you something, Fong?"

"The things you find are always interesting to me," replied Fong. He grinned because Tulio had been bringing him peculiar items since he was a child. Tulio was not aware of it, but Fong had saved everything that the boy had brought him.

"This is not a thing, Fong. Watch." Tulio threw his staff in the way he had earlier. Not only did it fly straight, but the staff also stuck in the ground, surprising the two of them.

"That is remarkable, Tulio. I have never heard of anyone who has propelled a tool or a staff without spinning." Fong walked to the staff with Tulio.

"Our people and other humans have had tools and weapons for many generations. With the exception of the staff, they are small, like the axe or stone knife. When the tools are thrown, they spin through the air. How did you learn to hurl your staff in that way?" Fong sat on a stone and looked at Tulio, who had picked up his staff. The boy told him the story of what happened at the pool in the stream.

"You have been most successful," suggested Fong. "Learning to swim like a wolf and handle a staff as you did are remarkable feats. Rarely has a person accomplished so much so quickly. Do you think you can teach me your technique?"

Because Fong was so familiar with tools and weapons, it did not take him long to master how to throw the staff. As he practiced, his mind was working.

"Tulio, I think your staff could be used for hunting if it had a sharper tip." Fong selected a cutting stone and shaved the tip of the staff. He threw it, and the staff stuck in the ground.

Taking the staff to his fire, Fong heated the pointed tip for a moment. "This will make the tip a little harder," he told Tulio. He and Tulio threw the staff a few more times, and in most cases, the tip stuck in the ground.

Then Fong had another idea. He looked at his collection of tools, which was the largest in the clan. Among the tools was a flint knife approximately the length of a man's hand. The end was bound with leather strips so it could be gripped tightly without

77

cutting the user's hand. He lifted the knife and held it near the tip of the staff.

Satisfied with what he saw, Fong unwrapped the leather strips from the knife. With another cutting tool, he made a slit in the end of the staff. He cut the wood carefully so the staff would not split. It took some time for him to do this, but Tulio waited patiently. He had seen Fong make tools in the past and was fascinated by how it was done. He had assimilated skills connected with tool making from Fong, but he was far less talented than the older man.

Completing the slit in the staff, Fong put the handle of the flint knife in it. He wrapped the leather strips around the staff to hold the knife. Doubting the security of the binding, he undid his work and removed the knife. He made chips in the handle of the knife, replaced it in the slit, and wrapped the leather strips around the staff again. The chips in the knife made the leather strips hold more reliably. He reinforced his work with more leather strips to be sure the knife would remain in place and showed the finished tool to Tulio.

"This might be an effective hunting staff," said Tulio. "If I can throw it accurately, the staff will make hunting easier and safer, especially for big animals. You have an inventive mind, Fong, and I am grateful for your help."

"Thank you, but remember, it was you who learned to hurl the staff. I simply made an improvement to your discovery. We also do not know how well it will work. You and I should try your hunting staff before we begin bragging about it. We can do that on another day. For now, forget the staff and go to your family. Lakus and Nasha might not have eaten everything yet."

As Tulio turned to go, he saw Maddia and Nasha coming his way. "Is something wrong, sister?" he inquired, not expecting to see them.

"Yes, you are delaying our dinner. Mother sent me to fetch you. You are welcome, too, Fong. We are fortunate to have an abundance of fish. Lakus will tell you the details when you see him." She looked at the staff that Fong grasped. "Why did you make an implement that is so similar to a spear plant?"

Fong and Tulio looked at the staff with new eyes. She was correct. With the stone knife as a point, the staff had the shape of the spear of an asparagus plant. The asparagus was one of the clan's most prized foods during the spring and was enjoyed by humans wherever it flourished. When it emerged from the earth, the shoot had no leaves and was just a thick, green stalk with a cluster of buds at the top. It was usually cooked by roasting in the fire or wrapped in leaves and steamed. Eventually, the asparagus spear grew and looked like many other plants. In its mature form, it was not very palatable.

"You have humbled us, Maddia," laughed Fong. "Tulio and I were becoming prideful about our brilliant creation. Perhaps your naming it for a common plant will help us recall that vanity is not an attractive trait. As for your mother's invitation to dinner, I will accept with gratitude."

When they arrived at Maddia's shelter, Tulio and Fong did not expect to see so many friends and family participating in the evening meal. Even more unusual was the number of fish roasting beside the fire.

"Where did these fish come from?" asked Tulio. "It is a welcome surprise."

Hearing the question, Lakus and Salora, a girl about the same age, rushed over. "We caught the fish this afternoon," answered Lakus. "It was easy."

"It was not easy," said Salora. "It was lucky, and you know it."

Lakus tried to make an angry face at Salora, but he giggled when Salora rolled her eyes. The girl with flaming red hair explained what happened.

"We went to the lower pool to catch fish. Lakus brought a basket he had made to carry the fish home. As you know, he does not enjoy handling fish." Salora gave Lakus a little push, and he shrugged his shoulders.

"Lakus took the basket into the water and placed it at the end of the pool. It started to float off, so Lakus put rocks in the basket. The rocks kept a portion of the basket under the water, and it did not float away."

Salora tried to continue, but Lakus interrupted her. "In the beginning, we caught only one fish. Salora wanted to put the fish in the basket, and when she got there, she saw it was already teeming with

Nasha, The First Dog

fish. They swam in circles in front of and inside the basket. She came back to get me and showed me the fish in the basket. We climbed out of the pool and walked to where the basket was. We proceeded slowly and were careful not to scare the fish. We pulled it up, and the basket had more fish than we could count."

"I think the fish tried to escape from us, but the basket was blocking part of the stream, and they could not swim any farther," added Salora. "Lakus dumped the fish on the bank and put it in the water again as he had before. We waded into the pool and splashed around. When we lifted the basket from the water, more fish had swum into it, as if they had been drawn there by magic."

Zibio joined Fong and Tulio and broke into the conversation. "Even though there are many fish, you two better get some quickly. When Lakus is not talking, he inevitably turns to eating."

As they walked toward the fire and the cooking fish, Tulio asked his father, "Is what Lakus said true? Using a basket to trap fish as he described would be a wonderful thing."

"I must assume he is telling the truth. I think there is no other way that he and Salora could have caught so many fish in such a short period of time," answered Zibio.

"I agree with Tulio," said Fong. "Lakus has stumbled upon a marvelously practical idea. I would not have thought to use a basket to trap fish." He contemplated the notion for a moment and then commented, "We should try this fish trap in different sections of the stream and the river. There is a caution to be mindful of, specifically for the stream that is close to our camp. We cannot take too many fish from the river or there will be none left for our future needs. It seemed impossible that we could catch all the fish, but with the fish trap, we may."

"We should discuss this with Baratho and the council of elders," advised Zibio. "But for now, I am more interested in seeing this spear you made. Maddia could not stop giggling when she told me of this fearsome weapon that has the form of an asparagus sprout."

Chapter 12

"How are you doing with your spear?" asked Maddia.

"Not as well as I wished," responded Tulio. "Fong and I have made several more, and I have practiced throwing them. So far, I have not been sufficiently skilled to hit a rabbit."

Patting Nasha on the head, Maddia said, "A rabbit may be too small and too fast to kill with a spear. A rabbit is more suitable prey for a young wolf."

A number of young people from the clan were on a foraging trip. A grove of fig trees was within hiking distance of the camp. Figs were a favored food of the clan. In addition to being tasty when eaten ripe, they could be cooked with many foods to improve their flavor. Humans had discovered that figs could be dried and kept through the winter when fresh fruit was not available. Because of the invention of the basket, more figs than ever would be brought to the camp.

The children of the clan loved harvesting figs because they got to eat the delicious fruit while they worked. It was a welcome treat, made more enjoyable because figs were among the earliest fruits to mature. No one in the clan had eaten new fruit since the fall.

The youngsters were accompanied by some of the women. The oldest boys in the party, including Tulio, carried weapons. No danger was expected, but the clans recognized that there were countless risks outside of camp, and they were prepared for the worst.

The day was warm and sunny, ideal for harvesting figs. The older children climbed the branches and dropped figs to the ground. The younger children put the figs in baskets, munching a few until their bellies were full. The women roamed among the fig trees, picking the low-hanging fruit and making sure none of the children fell from the trees.

By the time the sun was overhead, the baskets were overflowing. The women rounded up the children, but before they returned to camp, they decided to spend time at a pond fed by a tiny brook. The grass beside the pond had been nibbled by grazing animals, so it was short and soft. The spot was perfect for the children to play and the women to relax.

Tulio and Maddia paddled with Nasha in the water in the center of the pond. When the little children begged Tulio and Maddia to teach them how to paddle like Nasha, they came into the shallow water. With the aid of some of the women, they taught a handful of children how to swim. They made these children promise never to try it by themselves or to go out into deep or swift water. The children picked up the skill quickly but stayed close to the shore.

With everyone focusing on the new swimmers, they were unaware that mammoths had wandered from the forest into the fig trees. These elephant-like animals were more than twice the height of a human with a powerful trunk and long, curved tusks. Because of their enormous size, mammoths spent most of their time eating plants. The leaves and fruit of the fig trees were among their favorite foods, too.

Humans sometimes hunted mammoths. They would do so in groups, usually by trapping a lone mammoth in an enclosed space such as a canyon. Axes and large stones were thrown at the mammoth, and the hunting party hoped to kill the animal or wound it so severely that it could not escape. This was an inefficient and dangerous way to hunt, but the risk seemed worth it. A mammoth provided enough meat for weeks, and its skin, bones, and tusks were used for many purposes.

Mammoths were not aggressive animals, but their size alone made them a menace to humans. If a herd of mammoths stampeded or merely strolled through a camp, the beasts could destroy everything in their path. Individual mammoths were not usually a threat because humans could avoid them easily. The most serious risk existed when a human came near a group of mammoths and young animals were present.

Nasha was the first to notice the mammoths. Standing in the water, she sniffed the light breeze and scanned the area around the pond. Maddia saw that Nasha had quit playing and was staring at the grove of fig trees. Following Nasha's gaze, she saw the mammoths.

"Be quiet, please," whispered Maddia and pointed toward the trees.

Everyone was silent and stopped what they were doing at once. The members of the clan understood that their survival depended on being alert to danger and reacting in the correct way. In this case, being still and quiet was the best thing to do because they did not want to frighten the mammoths.

Although mammoths were plant eaters and normally preferred to avoid humans, Tulio sensed that they were in jeopardy. He could see that there were baby mammoths in the group, so the adults would be protective. The ground beside the pond was flat and open, offering no place to hide. What was more dismaying was the realization that the trail to the camp was inaccessible because it was beyond the fig trees.

"Keep Nasha by your side," whispered Tulio. "She might startle the mammoths if they see her."

The children left the water calmly and stood by their mothers. Ganni and the women tried to calm the children, and he said to Tulio, "Do you have any ideas? I am worried that the mammoths might come our way in order to drink after they have eaten."

Tulio knew the area well. He began drawing a map in the dirt. "Here we are," he pointed out, "and here are the mammoths. The path we have to take to the camp is beyond the fig trees. If we can get to the cliff beside the fig trees, we can climb up. It is too steep for the mammoths. We can try to make our way to camp along the top of the ridge, which is harder, or we can wait until the mammoths have finished eating and return on the easier trail."

"Look how far it is to the cliff," said Ganni. "I am not confident we can make it without being seen by the mammoths."

"You are probably right," said Tulio. "You and I can create a diversion. While the others go toward the cliff, you and I can head in the other direction. If we make a little noise, the mammoths might ignore the women and children and focus on us. When they come our way, the chances are good that we can get to the hills over there." He pointed to a rise beyond the pond. "I know of some caves in which we can conceal ourselves."

"Nasha and I will lend a hand," insisted Maddia. "Nasha will not be in any danger because she is faster than the mammoths. If need be, I can go into the pond and swim to the deep water if I do not think I can make it to the caves."

Neither of the boys favored her plan, but they were unable to convince Maddia to escape with the women and children. The truth of the matter was that they were relieved to have her join them. Nasha might be invaluable if the mammoths discovered them, and Maddia was bright and fearless.

Led by Belia and Leeza, the women and children walked slowly toward the cliff. When they were at the halfway point, Tulio, Ganni, and Maddia went the opposite way. Maddia kept Nasha close to her.

The women and children were at the cliff and climbed up the steep slope. All of them made it to the high ground. Seeing that those on the cliff were no longer in jeopardy, Ganni interrupted Tulio and Maddia.

"The mammoths have not yet spotted us. Let us flee to the cliffs," suggested Ganni. "I think we can reach them even if the mammoths see us."

Both Tulio and Maddia agreed with Ganni. They turned and walked back as quietly as they could. They had not gone far when they heard the rumble of the mammoth warning sound. A large male had detached himself from the group and was lumbering toward them.

The three of them ran toward the cliff. The mammoth turned slightly and continued to chase them. They were surprised at how quickly it moved for an animal so immense. Because it had been on the far side of the fig grove, it was now between them and the cliffs.

"Stay together," shouted Ganni, who had slowed down. Maddia and Tulio joined him. Nasha put herself between the three of them and the mammoth, which had halted and now had its back to the cliff.

The mammoth lifted its massive head, bellowed, and rushed forward. It stopped about fifty paces from the humans and the wolf. The mammoth tossed its head back and forth and pawed the earth.

"It does not know what to do," said Maddia. "Maybe we should split up and try the original plan again. One of us can distract the mammoth, and the rest can escape to the cliffs. When they are at the cliff, they can try to keep the mammoth's attention. Nasha and I will be the decoys."

Without thinking of her own welfare, Maddia and Nasha bolted toward the pond. Tulio tried to grab her, but she was too fast. Glancing with concern at his brave yet foolish sister, he and Ganni ran in the direction of the cliff.

The mammoth turned and charged toward Maddia. Seeing this, Nasha did what any wolf would do and circled behind the mammoth. The beast cut short its attack and turned toward Nasha, who was facing the mammoth and growling.

A single wolf is no threat to a mammoth, nor could a mammoth do much harm to a wolf, which is faster and more agile. The animals were acting according to their natures. So, too, were Tulio and Ganni. They could not run and leave Maddia and Nasha. The two boys sprinted toward the mammoth and began yelling. Without thinking, Tulio let the spear fly. For the first time, he hit what he was aiming at, and the spear lodged in the mammoth's shoulder.

The spear did not injure the mammoth gravely,

but it was a painful irritation. The mammoth turned from Nasha in the direction of the spear and tried to extract the annoyance with its trunk. Seeing what happened, Maddia scurried toward her brother and Ganni, with Nasha close on her heels. Because the spear distracted the mammoth, they were able to flee to the cliff and scramble to safety.

Shaking its shoulders and legs furiously, the mammoth dislodged the spear. When it spun around to face its attackers, they had disappeared. It turned several times to satisfy itself that the area was clear. Believing that the danger had passed, the mammoth ambled toward the herd, which was leaving the grove of fig trees and shuffling to the pond for a drink and a wallow.

The women and children looked with admiration at the three young people and the wolf who had risked their lives for them. Had the mammoths not been nearby, they would have chanted the ancient words of celebration and thanks. They did not want to disturb the animals, which seemed to have forgotten about the humans. Instead, they made their way silently across the top of the cliff until they were out of sight of the mammoths. Reaching the edge of the cliff, they glanced back at the mammoths. The animals had found the baskets they had left behind in their haste to escape and were eating the figs as well as the fresh willow twigs of which the baskets had been made just the day before. Laughing, the group climbed down to the trail that would take them back to camp. They would have an extraordinary tale to tell by the communal fire that evening, a tale with danger, bravery, and a very funny ending.

Chapter 13

"Here is another spear to replace the one you lost yesterday," said Fong, handing a new weapon to Tulio. It was the next day, and Tulio had gone to the toolmaker's shelter with Maddia and Nasha.

"You should have seen Tulio throw the spear," said Maddia. "It flew like a bird straight to the mammoth. I have never seen anything comparable."

"We shall discuss what happened at another time," remarked Fong. "Using spears might be a better method for us to hunt mammoths. The way we do it now is clumsy and dangerous. Come, let me show you what I have constructed."

Fong led them to the fire pit in the rear of his shelter. Beside it he had piled rocks in a curious way. The mound was the height of a grown man and had the form of a hill, with a tapering top and broad base. There was an opening at the top where smoke could escape and another at the bottom where wood could be inserted. A large stone was in the middle of the bottom.

"Melting the golden stones got me thinking. Putting a fire within a stack of rocks will make it hotter, and things other than the golden stones might melt. If they do not melt, they might be modified in a useful way." Fong walked around the stones and repositioned some of them. "I will build a fire inside the rocks. I can put things on the flat rock in the middle and see if they melt."

"What makes you think these different substances may be transformed?" inquired Maddia.

"Ice melts into water, and the golden stone changed shape when it was put in the fire. The sap of evergreen trees is liquid when it initially seeps from the bark, but as it dries, it becomes harder." Fong picked up a length of pine wood. "Look at the sap on this piece of wood. It is hard, almost like a stone. Yet when the log is burned, the sap turns soft before it ignites."

"So why did you have us come here?" asked Tulio.

"I would like you to help me collect different rocks. We will spend the morning seeking rocks that have odd colors and texture. There might also be other things that we can test with heat. When we return, we will put them in the fire and see what happens. I have spoken with your families, and they have given me permission to ask you." Fong looked at them hopefully. Their cooperation would make the job of collecting rocks easier than if he had to do it alone.

"We would be honored to assist you," answered Tulio, and Maddia shook her head in agreement. "There are others who might want to go. May they join us?"

"That would be most welcome," replied Fong. "There are many kinds of rocks. Your friends can make the work go faster. Be sure to ask their parents before inviting them. There are many chores to be done, and I do not want to take children from their responsibilities."

Maddia and Nasha went to the main part of the camp, where she told her friends about working with Fong. She discussed the adventure with their parents, and it was not long before she had assembled an enthusiastic group, including her brother, Lakus. Each of them brought a basket to carry their stones. If they were fortunate, they might discover extra food they could eat for the meal later.

While they waited for Maddia, Tulio and Fong discussed trading with clans in the area. Fong's tools were prized by the clans, and he traded them for animal skins, shells from sea animals, food, and various articles that the clan required. Tulio listened attentively while Fong described the individuals they traded with, where they met, and how to value the goods that were exchanged. Baratho and Zibio were the chief traders for the clan, but it was critical that all of those involved in making or collecting the traded goods were familiar with the process. It was equally necessary that the young people who were verging on adulthood should learn how to conduct trade.

With Maddia and the children present, Tulio explained to them what they would be looking for. It was not difficult, but it was important to get as many different rocks as possible. The children did this easily, and while they were finding rocks, Fong looked for items that might be affected by the heat of a fire. Tulio and Nasha patrolled the area around the searchers, but fortunately, there were no dangers.

At sunset, the group strolled into camp with full baskets. They had gathered an amazing variety of stones, which the children left at Fong's shelter. They went to their families, eager to tell stories of what they had experienced.

Fong looked over the hundreds of rocks that were in baskets by his shelter. They came in many colors, and some were unfamiliar to Fong. He was very pleased with what the children had done. Maddia queried him about what he would do next.

"When the opportunity presents itself, I will try to melt the stones. It will take many days to put all the stones in the fire, but there is no hurry. In this case, I think that patient observation will be essential. I have plenty of duties to occupy my time."

"For now," he continued, "the three of us can identify the rocks that look interesting." He handed each of them a basket and said, "Look thoroughly at the rocks. If you see anything unusual, point it out to me. I do not know if we can tell ahead of time how a rock will respond in the fire, but I also do not think anyone in the clan has considered rocks for this purpose."

While the three of them went through their baskets of rocks, Nasha curled up at Maddia's feet. Though she had grown in size, she was still a pup in many ways. The day had been prolonged and filled with activity, and she was exhausted.

Maddia was the first to identify something with puzzling characteristics. "Look at this, Fong." she said. "Is it a golden stone?"

She handed the rock to Fong, who examined it meticulously. The greenish rock had flecks of a substance that compared to golden stones, but it was more orange than gold. "Because it is so atypical, this is one of the stones we shall put in the fire first. Well done, my sharp-eyed girl."

Hearing approaching footsteps, Nasha woke instantly and trotted defensively to the front of Fong's shelter. The welcoming tone of her whine indicated that someone familiar had arrived. Leeza followed Nasha to where Fong, Tulio, and Maddia were sitting.

"What is that collection of rocks?" she asked, staring at the structure that Fong had built. "It is a strange cooking hearth."

"I have not decided what to call it yet," said Fong, "but its purpose is to hold a unique type of fire. I am hoping that the stones will retain the heat and make the fire hotter than if it were open. It took an uncommonly hot fire to melt the golden stones."

"I was told of your collection of rocks and how you want to see what happens to them in a fire. I want you try this in the fire, too." Leeza handed

Fong a lump of mud that had been molded by hand so it looked like a shell.

"When we take shellfish from the river, the shape of the shell often remains in the mud. When the river is low, the shapes become hard as they dry in the sun. Maybe the mud will change in the fire. I molded this piece of mud to resemble a shell," said Leeza. "We have used shells for tools and for drinking for many generations. I tried before to make a shell shape with mud and use it for the same purposes, but it always fell apart. This time, I put the mud in the bottom of a basket and let it dry. Can you see how the texture of the basket has been transferred to the outside of the shape?"

Looking at the clay shell, Fong added, "Yes, I recall that you mentioned this to me before. Sometimes when a fire is finished, the dirt under it is harder than it was before the fire was made. I did not give it much thought. I like your idea."

"I remember building shapes with river clay when I was a child," said Tulio. "We would make animals, fish, and birds. We put them in the sun to dry. They broke easily, and when it rained on them, they got soft. None of them resembled animals closely, but it was fun to make them."

"It is too late to light the fire today," said Fong. "A long time is needed for the flames to get hot enough to melt rocks. Let us begin in the morning. I hope all of you will come tomorrow to see what happens. If you have made any figures of river clay, bring them and we will put them in the fire."

Fong amassed extra wood that evening and lit the fire in the pile of rocks as soon as the sun came up. By the middle of the morning, it had grown hotter than any fire he had ever made. A group of children and adults from the clan had come together to see what he would do.

The initial challenge that confronted Fong was embarrassing. The fire became so hot that he could not get near enough to put any stones inside the hearth. Griffo suggested that he put the stones on an axe and slide them onto the flat rock within the fire, which Fong tried. It worked, but the process was clumsy. While the stones sat in the fire, Fong adapted Griffo's recommendation. He took the tip of a spear he had made and replaced it with a digging tool that was broader. This wider tool had an extended handle, and with it, he could slip stones in and out of the fire smoothly.

Fong extracted the heated stone from the fire. He saw no changes, other than blackness from the fire. He put the stone in an empty basket by Maddia and asked her to keep the tested stones separate from those that were untested. The girl felt gratified by being chosen for this job.

The next rock to be investigated was the greenish one that Maddia had unearthed. Fong inserted it into the center the fire and waited. While he waited, Fong selected some of the clay shapes and prepared to put them in the fire. He decided on this because several of the children had brought figures they had made, and it would make them feel they were essential to the success of the process.

Because of the flames, Fong could not see what happened to the green rock he had put in the fire. When he removed it, he was positive that it was different from when it had been inserted. The rock had been altered a little, and there were more orange flecks. The rock was too hot to handle, but he pointed at it and said to Maddia, "Your green rock has been reshaped by the fire. When it cools, we shall look at it more closely."

While Maddia's rock cooled, Fong put Leeza's clay shape in the fire with figures that the children made. It didn't take long for something to occur. The shape in the hottest part of the fire exploded into many pieces. With the new tool, Fong quickly pushed the others to a cooler spot in the fire. Fearing another explosion, he left them in for just a short time.

As Fong pulled the clay shapes from the fire, he could feel that they had been affected. They seemed harder and lighter on the tool than when he had inserted them. Before they had cooled to the touch, he tapped them with a stone knife. The shapes made a distinctive noise that was different from what they had sounded like before. The fire had changed the clay in a way that had not been anticipated.

After giving the clay shapes time to cool, Fong picked them up one at a time. He appraised each shape, hefted it in his hand, and returned it to the child who had made it. The final shape he touched was Leeza's. He passed it to her, and she turned it in her hand while smiling at Fong. She held his arm fondly and said, "Thank you, Fong. You are truly a worker of miracles. Only you could have foreseen that firing the river clay could have had such a result. I will do my best to put your discovery to good use."

In the succeeding days, Fong evaluated many stones. He learned that some of the stones produced substances similar to the golden stones but of different colors. He would study these, and with the passage of time, subsequent generations of toolmakers would devise ways of making them into implements that had not been seen before. No person in the clan could imagine how the stones that Fong heated in his fire would affect them and the rest of humans.

Chapter 14

The elders of the clan met at the end of the fall, a tradition that Baratho had initiated in his first year as leader. When they had taken their positions in the great hut, he asked their opinions about the most sensible course of action for the coming winter. The clan could stay in the valley or trek to another place where food might be more plentiful. There were risks involved in both choices.

"Because of Leeza's baskets, we have collected and stockpiled more food than ever before. If we conserve what we have accumulated and hunt through the winter, we can probably survive here until at least spring." Baratho's voice had an optimistic tone as he continued. "We were fortunate to come upon this valley last year, and we may have to relocate in the coming year. For the sake of our children, I suggest keeping the camp here for another winter. What do you think of this proposal?"

With hardly any exceptions, the elders agreed

with Baratho. They would remain in the valley through the winter. No enemy clans had come their way, and their food stores were adequate. The basket trap would let them catch fish through the winter, since the river did not freeze over completely. Because of Nasha's abilities, they might be more proficient at hunting fresh meat than before. It would not be very much, for many of the animals migrated away in winter, but they would pull through.

Life in the camp during winter was simple but demanding. Families spent the majority of the time in their huts. On warm days, they would search for dried fruit that still hung on the trees and nuts that they had missed on earlier foraging trips. The hunters left the camp each day, but they were often futile. The women and children tried to catch fish, but this was unpleasant work that produced little. Their food usually came from what they had stored.

Winter days were not wasted. Families cut willow twigs and made baskets. They had more baskets than they could use, but baskets could be traded with neighboring clans. They also cut hide into strips that could be used for binding, made clothes from animal fur, and collected wood for fires.

With his helpers, Fong studied more stones in the fire. It was tedious work that was frustrating. A sizable quantity of wood had to be collected to keep the fire hot, and few of the stones changed in any way. Despite this, Fong and those who supported him kept at the task. They did not know how the material that seemed to melt from the stones could be used, but they were convinced that it would be significant for the clan.

An outcome that Fong had not predicted was what happened to the wax made by bees. Humans had been eating honey for countless years. Bees stored honey in waxy clusters in their hives. Humans squeezed the honey from the waxy clusters, which were then discarded.

Fong put a piece of bees' wax in the fire and was astounded by what he saw. The wax melted almost immediately and then started to burn. Once it went into the fire, there was no way he could get any of it out because it melted so rapidly. He was not sure what to do with this information, but he thought that any substance that burned so quickly would eventually prove to be useful.

Many families were making things using river clay. With continuing practice, Fong devised a way of baking the clay shapes in his stone fireplace and make them harder than before. At the outset, most of the shapes were playthings made by children. Leeza, however, made an article with the appearance of a small basket and called it a bowl.

She began with a lump of clay and pushed her fist into the middle. With her fingers, she brought the sides up to make them higher and thinner. The work was painstaking, and it took her many hours to find the right clay and to develop a technique that made the correct shape.

The object that Leeza made had the shape of a

basket, but because it was made of hardened clay, it could hold water and food without leaking. When the clan saw what Leeza had done, they wanted to make bowls for themselves. Leeza demonstrated to them how to do this, and many people in the clan made their own bowls. They came in various sizes and shapes, and like baskets, the bowls were used for innumerable purposes.

It was during the winter that one of the clan's most consequential discoveries was made. As was frequently the case, it was an accident.

Late in the season, as the days were getting longer, Maddia sat with Nasha beside the fire. She and Lakus were picking loose hair from Nasha, who loved the attention she was receiving. Nasha's coat had grown thick during the winter, and they were surprised by the amount of fur that she shed.

"Look at this," said Lakus. He tugged a clump of fur from Nasha and rubbed his hands together. The fur quickly became a strand. "Can you make a strand longer than mine?" He gave Maddia a strand of Nasha's fur that was the length of his hand. It was made of many individual hairs that had become entwined.

Rising to the challenge, Maddia picked up a handful of Nasha's fur that was on the floor of the shelter. She worked the fur as Lakus had. The clump of fur formed a shorter, thicker strand. To her brother's glee, Maddia acknowledged that he had created a longer strand.

"What have you two done?" asked Belia curiously.

She closely appraised both of the strands the children had made. The long strand pulled apart easily, but the short strand did not. Belia picked up a tuft of Nasha's fur from the floor and rubbed it between her hands, observing what happened as she did. She was able to turn the fur into a strand. She then picked up another tuft, attached it to the end of the strand, and continued the process. Belia repeated this again and again until she had a strand that was as long as her arm.

"Mother seems to have won the game," said Maddia. She then asked, "How did you manage to do that?"

Belia showed them how she made a short strand and joined bits of fur to the end of it. She did it several times, and in a while, she had a strand that was longer than she was tall. It was not very strong, but she had an idea. If the strands were wound together, they would be most likely be stronger.

Until this discovery, the clan had only a handful of binding materials. Hides could be cut into strips, and grass could be used to tie small things together. Long hairs from animals could be used for some purposes, as could vines and pieces of certain plants. None of them had the versatility of the strand made from Nasha's fur.

"Lakus, what made you think of this?" asked Belia.

"I did not think of it," answered Lakus sheepishly. "I could not get Nasha's hair off my hand, and it was making me itch. When I rubbed my hands together, the fur just stuck together. I could then take it off easily."

Belia put her arms around Lakus and hugged him. She recalled a number of the plants she knew and wondered of she might do the same thing with parts of them. When summer returned, she would try.

The next morning, a group of children and adults made their way to the story cave. It was a large cave not far from the camp. The walls of the cave were covered with paintings that told the clan's history.

In generations past, the clans told stories by the fire, but they did not draw pictures to represent the events. They were too busy surviving, and they were not aware of the variety of colors that nature could provide. This generation of humans in many clans was more efficient than ever before and expended less effort on seeking food. They had more time to explore things like drawing and other forms of art. Telling their stories by painting on cave walls or cutting into rocks had become a ritual followed by humans in many places.

Clan members of every age went to the story cave. Checo was among them, and he played a central role. He told a clan story, and those with him drew pictures that matched his words. The pictures were drawn with pigments made from plants, crushed stones, and clay. These colors were also used by humans to paint themselves for special occasions.

It had snowed the night before but the day was warming. There was a surprising amount of snow on the ground from previous storms. The path to the cave went beside a cliff, above which was a snowfield. It was a beautiful sight, with huge drifts of snow above the trail and a meadow below.

Because the path on the edge of the cliff was narrow, Maddia gripped the front of Checo's staff while he held the back. Lakus was behind Checo, and he described the path as they progressed. He would identify things like stones or roots that might cause Checo to trip. They were behind the main group as they crossed the path because Checo had to exercise greater caution than those who could see.

Without warning, the massive drifts of snow above the trail gave way with a roar. Such a snow slide was not abnormal at this time of the year because the snow was wet and heavy. It tumbled down on the path with incredible force.

Driven by panic, Nasha bolted along the path and escaped the avalanche. Maddia, seeing that the cliff had a slight overhang, pushed Checo and Lakus to safety against the rock wall. In so doing, she was exposed to the falling snow, which knocked her down and swept her from the trail. In an instant, she was gone, buried under tons of snow.

Checo and Lakus were unhurt, though the two of them were covered with loose snow. Those in front were fortunate to be out of the path of the slide. Nasha stood between Griffo and Belia and looked back. For the first time since being rescued, she was without Maddia. She lifted her head and howled mournfully.

With tentative steps, Nasha walked to the last place she had seen Maddia. She paced back and forth on the path, made even narrower by the slide. She caught Maddia's scent and leaped from the path into the fallen snow.

Belia sidled along the rock wall until she could grab Checo. She took his hand and told Lakus to take his other hand. She led them along the ledge to where the path was wider. Both of them were shaken but uninjured.

Nasha was digging furiously in the snow where signs of Maddia were the strongest. Understanding what Nasha was doing, Griffo made his way through the fallen snow and began digging with the wolf using his spear. Realizing that it was fruitless to keep digging in such deep snow, he turned the spear over and poked the blunt end into the snow.

Despite being buried under more than six feet of snow, Maddia was fortunate. She had landed on all fours, so there was a pocket of air below her. She could not budge, but Maddia could at least breathe. As she became more aware of what happened, fear began to envelop her. To her dismay, she was surrounded by blackness. The snow, although appearing white from above, blocked most of the light from reaching her eyes.

Through the snow, Maddia heard Nasha's muffled howl. A moment later, she heard the sound of digging. She attempted to cry out, but snow partially filled her mouth, and she could not take a breath. Nor could she shift her arms to clear the snow from her mouth. What was worse was the cold. Maddia had never experienced cold such as this in her life, and there was nothing she could do to lessen it except to sleep.

On the surface of the snow, Nasha was digging and Griffo was poking with the butt of his spear. He was feeling powerless, knowing how miserable Maddia must feel. He jerked his spear out of the snow and moved closer to Nasha. He found the deepest part of the hole she was digging and shoved his spear into it. At the depth of half his spear, he encountered something firm and prayed it was Maddia.

"Come here," he shouted. "I may have found her." Throwing his spear aside, he started digging with his hands alongside of Nasha.

Despite being soaked, Lakus went to assist Griffo, as did Ganni. Others wanted to participate, but there was no room for them to dig. It was slow going because of the texture of the snow and the unstable footing. Every so often, the snow on the sides would collapse, making their job more frustrating.

Yelping several times, Nasha dug more frantically. It was only a short time before she uncovered Maddia's tunic. Griffo stretched down and grasped the fur she was wearing. Pulling up gently, he loosened the snow around her. With a firm tug, he uncovered her head and shoulders. Maddia's face was bluish, and she was barely breathing.

"Lakus, dig around her legs. I am going to try to drag her out of the snow." Griffo could now put his hands under Maddia's arms and tug with more force. Lakus clawed the snow from around her legs, and Griffo freed the motionless girl.

"Belia, what can we do?" begged Griffo.

"It will take too much time to carry her to camp while she is this cold," reasoned Belia. "Let us make a fire. Who has the fire stones?"

"I have them," said Ganni, "and Tulio has the torches and dried grass. We should be able to make a fire quickly."

Ganni had the fire stones because it was necessary to have a fire in the cave. The fire and torches would make the cave sufficiently bright to create the paintings. The inside of the cave was dark, particularly in the far corners where the wall was more flat. Fire stones are two different kinds of stones that made sparks when they are struck together. The sparks would ignite the grass, which was soft and dry so it burned easily. When the grass ignited and a few twigs were added, the small flame could be used to light the torches.

While Ganni and Tulio made a fire, Belia begged for some clothes for Maddia. She unwrapped a fur she wore, and Lakus gave her his outer fur. Checo offered his tunic, which had not been dampened much by the snow. Belia objected, but Checo insisted, saying, "Maddia saved me. It is a trivial inconvenience for me to suffer the cold in order to make her more comfortable. I can stay by the fire."

Once her wet clothes were off and Maddia was wrapped in dry furs, Griffo and Belia carried her to the fire. It was small but would soon be bigger and hotter. Belia drew Maddia next to her to share her body heat, and Nasha rested her head on the girl's lap.

Maddia was aware of none of this. In her dream, she was tumbling from the cliff, everything looked white, and then it grew black. She felt terribly cold and was powerless to do anything. Then she experienced a floating sensation, and the darkness ended. She became warmer, and she smelled Belia's fragrance. It was a comfortable feeling that reminded her of when she was a little girl being held in her mother's arms. She was conscious of Nasha lying on her, and she stroked the wolf's fur.

When Maddia woke from her dream, Nasha was licking her face. She was in her mother's arms, and she was cozy and out of harm's way. A fire roared nearby, and surrounding her were the important people in her life.

"We thought you had gone from us, my child, but you have come back," said Belia, and tears of joy trickled down her cheeks.

Chapter 15

For the days immediately following the avalanche, Maddia spent most of her time in the family hut. Belia stayed with her to make sure the girl was fine. Nasha, of course, would not let Maddia out of her sight. The two of them would take brief walks outside, but otherwise, they rested in the hut.

On one of the outings, Nasha went up to a low bush and began rubbing against it. Maddia watched as the wolf used the branches to remove the fur she was shedding. As winter was coming to a close, Nasha's thick coat was beginning to fall off. The wolf would lean toward the bush and shift from front to back. Each time she did, more of her fur stuck to the thorny branches. She seemed relieved to have the fur gone, as if it had been bothering her.

After Nasha had finished, Maddia collected the loose fur that had stuck to the thorny branch. She was amazed at the quantity of fur that Nasha had shed. Maddia broke off the branches and brought them to the hut.

"Mother, look at all the fur from Nasha. She worked it loose on these branches." Maddia put the wolf fur down and showed her mother the thorny branches.

"I have seen clumps of fur on branches before, but I did not know where it came from. I cannot believe that Nasha could have rubbed against this branch without hurting herself." Belia explored the branch with her hands and felt the thorns. They were not so sharp as she originally had imagined. They had probably been worn down by weather and humans or animals passing by.

Belia broke the longest branch in half. She knelt down beside Nasha, who was lying on the ground. With a gentle stroke, Belia drew the branch through Nasha's coat. As she expected, the thorns on the branch picked up pieces of fur.

"What are you doing, mother?" asked Maddia.

"I wanted to see how Nasha managed to get her fur off without being hurt. I think she slid in just one direction." Belia stroked the wolf and loosened more of Nasha's fur. The wolf enjoyed the combing and uttered a contented sigh.

In a short time, Belia had accumulated a surprising amount of fur. She put it with the fur that Maddia had brought back. She observed, "Nasha's fur is very soft, and it keeps her warm. There is almost surely a way we can use it." She reflected on the idea and then stated, "In my many years, I have never thought of using simply the fur of an animal.

We have always used the hide of the animal with the fur attached for clothing. Why did we not think to lift the fur off and do something with it?"

"It must not be an easy thing to do," answered Maddia. "Not many animals have fur that falls off like Nasha's."

The wolf had rolled over, which gave Belia a chance to brush her fur on the other side with the branch. Each stroke loosened more fur, and before long, there was a large pile on the floor. As before, Nasha loved being pampered.

Belia looked at the thorny branch thoroughly. She then motioned for Maddia to sit with her on the floor of the hut. The girl had an exceedingly full head of unruly hair that was curly. Belia regularly ran her fingers through her daughter's hair to clean it and to prevent big tangles from forming. It was a practice observed by all the clans.

Hesitantly, Belia pulled the thorny branch through Maddia's hair. She was careful to do it tenderly and to touch only a few hairs at a time. She brushed Maddia's hair repeatedly. Many of the tangles came out easily, at least more easily than if she had tried to do it with her fingers. Maddia's hair was less disorderly, and the small pieces of twig and leaf were gone.

"How does that feel, Maddia?" asked Belia.

"Not as nice as when you touch my hair with your hands," replied the girl, "but not too bad. Why did you do it?"

"The thorny branch did such a good job with

Nasha that I tried it on your hair. You are aware of how hard it is to keep our hair clean and untangled. This method may be a better way to do it than with my fingers or the small stick I sometimes use."

The stick that Belia mentioned was about the same size as her finger. It had a sharpened tip, and she would use it to unravel the difficult tangles in Maddia's hair. The grooming stick was a traditional tool that the women in the family had relied on for generations.

"Does it make my hair look different?" wondered Maddia.

"Yes, it looks different, but it will not be evident to most people because I did the back of your head. We should try it when we are at the stream. I will work on the hair in the front of your head. You can examine your reflection in the water to see for yourself how it looks. But enough discussion of your hair. Let us see what we can do with Nasha's fur."

Belia laid the stick down and put the mound of wolf hair between the two of them. As she did before, Belia held some hair in her hands and twisted them together with her hands. The hair formed a strand, and she picked up more hair and attached it to the end. In no time she had a strand of wolf hair that reached from her head to the ground.

"You should do a strand," Belia said to Maddia. She handed the pile of fur to her daughter and stood up. While Maddia worked with the fur, Belia looked for the strand she had made before. She located it in a basket in the corner and returned to sit beside Maddia.

Maddia completed her strand in a matter of minutes. Belia now had three strands of wolf hair that were the height of an adult. She handed the ends of the three strands to Maddia and had her hold them. Belia twisted the strands of fur together attentively, stopping often to check her work.

"What are you doing, mother?" asked Maddia. She nearly dropped the strands as she spoke.

"Pay attention, daughter," said Belia, smiling at Maddia. "You are a crucial part of this test. A single strand made of wolf hair is not very strong. It separates easily. If we wrap three of them together, maybe the thicker strand will be stronger."

Belia turned the three strands together again and again. She worked patiently and deliberately until she had a thicker strand that was as tall as Maddia.

"Hold tightly," Belia told Maddia. "I want to see how strong the strand really is."

Maddia clutched the strand with two hands. Belia began tugging, at first easily, not wanting her strand to fail. She gradually pulled harder, but the strand did not break.

"You did it, mother," said Maddia proudly. When she sensed her mother releasing pressure on the string, she let go. Immediately, the three strands unwound. Both of them looked glumly at the strands and then at each other.

Before Maddia could speak, Belia said, "It is not your fault, Maddia. I did not foresee the possibility of the strands coming undone. But look at them."

Belia pointed to the three strands, which had not unwound completely. "See how they are still curly and wound around one another? I think I know how to keep the strands together. Wait here for a moment."

Belia took the three strands outside. She soaked them in the spring not far from the shelter. She also found a smooth stick and went back to the hut.

"This time, let us do it right," said Belia as she sat down with Maddia. Belia tied a knot in the strand and handed the knotted end to Maddia.

"The strands are wet," said Maddia.

"Yes, I think the water will hold the strands together. When your hair gets wet, it becomes silkier and the individual hairs cling together. Nasha's fur is likely to change in a similar way. Grip the knot firmly."

Belia twisted the strands another time, and when she got to the end, she knotted it. She then took the smooth stick and wrapped the strand around it while Maddia held it. Belia concluded by tucking the strand's end under the last loop to keep it in place.

"We shall let this sit for a time and see what happens," said Belia. "Let us search for your father and brothers to see if their hunt for the evening meal was successful."

The next day, Maddia woke at dawn. She bundled up in furs and took Nasha out for a walk. By the time the two of them had finished and made their way to the shelter, the others were awake, too. Zibio had put pieces of wood on the fire, and the living space was getting warmer.

"May we look at the strands?" begged Maddia.

"I am as eager as you are, daughter," answered Belia with a sense of anticipation. "Yes, we can look at them now."

"What are you two talking about?" wondered Zibio.

"It is a complicated story that we will be happy to tell you shortly," replied Belia. "But before beginning, we have something to show you."

Belia went to the corner where she had put the wound strands. She turned and handed the wrapped stick to Maddia. Looking unsure of themselves, the two of them unwound the strands systematically. They stayed together.

"We did it, mother," said Maddia. "Look."

Belia grasped the strand in her hand. She pulled on it and confirmed that it was as strong as it was before. It did not unwind, and she breathed a sigh of relief. Her mind was already racing as she considered the things that she and the other clan members could do with strands made from animal hair.

Just as she set about telling Zibio the story of the strand, they heard someone approaching the hut. Lakus pushed the flap open and welcomed Murra.

"I hope I am not too early," she said as she stepped inside. "I saw Maddia and Nasha, and I wondered how she was doing."

"I am fine," answered Maddia, "and you are in

time to learn about what a wonderful thing mother and I accomplished yesterday."

"It is not as exciting as Maddia lets on," suggested Belia, "but I think you will judge it to be interesting."

Belia retold the story of the thorny branch, Nasha's fur, and how they had made the strand. She passed the strand to Murra, who examined it carefully. She was one of the women in the clan who had a special talent for making things out of hides and plant fibers.

"This is an elegant strand," said Murra. "It reminds me of the fibers from the hemp plant, but it is markedly softer. You said you made this strand by rubbing Nasha's fur between your hands." Murra paused and then asked, "Have you tried doing that with hemp fibers?"

"No, I never thought about it. Maddia, can you hand me the basket behind you?" Belia pointed to a big basket containing a pile of plant fibers. The hemp plant thrived all around the camp and throughout the region. Humans used the fibers from the outer layer of the plant for many purposes because they were strong and flexible. If stripped from the plant correctly, a fiber might be as long as a person's arm and could be used to tie things together.

Belia took some of the hemp fibers and worked them with her hands as she had the fur from Nasha. The hemp was too stiff, so it did not form a strand like Nasha's fur had. She looked disappointed.

119

"Hand me a few pieces of the hemp," said Murra. "You said you twisted the three strands of Nasha's fur together. Maybe we can twist the hemp fibers together."

Murra took several hemp fibers and tied a knot in the end. She twisted them together, and they made a stronger strand. Remembering Belia's story, Murra took more fibers and included them. She did not only add them to the end, but mixed them near the middle of the strand. As she twisted them, the fibers held together, forming a thicker strand.

Understanding what Murra was doing, Belia went outside and picked up another smooth stick. She returned to the shelter and wound the hemp strand onto the stick, being careful to put the knot under the initial turn of the strand so it would stay in place. As Murra added hemp to the strand and twisted it, Belia continued winding the strand on the stick.

In a short time, the two of them had used up all the hemp. They had made a strand that could have reached the roof of the shelter. The strand was wound on the stick, and Murra had knotted the end she held. Belia tucked it under the last turn on the stick.

"Let me soak this in water," said Belia, and she left the shelter with the strand. When she had completed the task, she returned and handed Murra the wound hemp. "You can take this to your hut until tomorrow. If we are fortunate, the strands of hemp will cling together as well as Nasha's fur did. There is one Nasha, and she sheds just once a year, so her fur is of limited use. Hemp grows everywhere, and if we can twist its fibers together, we can make as many strands as we need."

"How can we use the hemp strands?" inquired Zibio.

"I am not sure," responded Murra, "but at the outset, we had no idea what to do with Leeza's baskets. Today, we cannot imagine how we got by without them."

Murra showed up early the following morning. In her hands was the strand of hemp. Twisting and soaking the hemp, then wrapping it on the stick, had kept the fibers together. When Belia saw it, she reminded Murra of what she had said the night before. Belia agreed with Murra that this way of using hemp would someday prove to be as useful as Leeza's baskets.

Chapter 16

The clan shared the region where they lived with a herd of aurochs, a grazing animal that ate grasses and other plants. In the summer, the horned beasts would climb up the hills to the top of the plateau. Food was plentiful there, and because the trees on the highlands were sparse, they could see danger coming. Babies were born in early summer and grew quickly.

When cold weather arrived, the aurochs would migrate down into the valley. They were less exposed to harsh weather in the valley, and they could find food throughout the winter. The aurochs were also more accessible in the valley to hunting animals like wolves, lions, and humans.

A considerable portion of the clan's meat came from the aurochs. If an aurochs could be killed, it would feed the whole clan for days. Hunting an aurochs, however, was dangerous. The animals were huge and often weighed more than ten humans.

They had enormous horns and could kill a hunter with a swift turn of their head.

Maddia, Piero, and Nasha set out on a fine morning to collect first greens. These were hardy plants that pushed through the soil in the earliest days of spring, sometimes appearing while snow was yet on the ground. In addition to being flavorful, the first greens were believed to prevent sicknesses that afflicted the clan at the conclusion of winter.

"Be careful, children," warned Belia. "You are not the only ones who are looking for first greens. The aurochs are not far off, and they are as fond of first greens as you are." Belia had become more protective of Maddia since her brush with death in the snow slide.

"We will stay away from the aurochs, Mother," sighed Maddia. She hoisted a basket that she had made that winter and handed another to Piero. The baskets were enormously practical to the clan, and although they had been invented recently, they had changed the way the clan lived. Piero and Maddia should be able to gather sufficient first greens to make a meal with the meat obtained by the hunters.

"Piero, keep a close eye on Maddia. Do not let Nasha do sentinel duties on her own." Ganni poked his brother affectionately.

Piero smiled, feeling a sense of pride in playing the role of Maddia's guardian. It was the first time that he was expected to do a job that was considered man's work. Though he was little more than a boy, Piero was zealous in fulfilling his assignment.

"We will collect an adequate amount of first greens," said Piero with a grin. "I am less confident that you and Griffo will return with meat for the clan. Maybe Nasha should be assisting you hunters."

"Let us go, Piero," said Maddia with feigned ridicule. "The hunters must be on their way quickly if they are to succeed. They are not as talented as they might be if they did less talking and more stalking."

Maddia and Piero walked away from the group of hunters. Nasha followed closely behind them. They joked with one another, but they were well aware that the clan required the food they would find today, and there were many dangers that they might face. Fierce lions, wolves, and bears were in many of the same places as humans, and for these animals, humans were prey.

"I think there should be many greens by the spring," said Piero. "I do not understand why, but the plants seem to grow better there."

"It might have something to do with the water," suggested Maddia. "Or possibly it is because the sun shines there in the winter. In any case, the rocks are warm on the coldest day if the sun strikes them."

The spring was actually a creek that fell down the face of a cliff. It tumbled through a crevice and emerged fifty feet above the two children. A pool formed at the base of the cliff, and the water ran into the stream that flowed by the camp. The tumbling waterfall was beautiful, and Maddia delighted in visiting the spot whenever she could.

In the winter, the sun shone directly on the

rocks. Because they were dark, they absorbed the energy of the sun and became warm. During the night, the rocks released this heat so the canyon had a slightly higher temperature than the more exposed areas.

When they reached the spring, they were pleased to see that the first greens were plentiful. They flourished on the flat ground by the pool and beside the stream. The two children set about at once filling their baskets, nibbling occasionally on the tasty plants they harvested.

Nasha paced around sniffing here and there. She was watchful for danger, looking in all directions and cocking her ears with every new sound. After wandering for a while not far from Maddia, Nasha found a cozy bed of dried grass and curled up for a nap.

Maddia and Piero continued their work. They chatted about unimportant matters, and as the sun climbed higher, they became tired. Fortunately, their baskets were close to being full, so they decided to return to the camp along the stream and pick more greens on the way.

"Nasha, it is time to leave." Maddia spoke softly so she wouldn't alarm the sleeping wolf. Nasha opened her eyes and uncurled her tail, which had been covering her nose, but she hardly stirred otherwise. She got up slowly, arched her back, and stretched her front paws in front of her. She walked to the spring, lapped the water, and then ambled to Maddia. The wolf pushed her head into the girl's hand, a signal that Maddia recognized. Nasha wanted her attention, and the girl obliged.

As she scratched Nasha's ears, Maddia uttered soothing words that Nasha seemed to understand. The wolf shut her eyes and let out a deep breath, showing that she loved what Maddia was doing to her.

"That is enough affection," said Piero in a kindly tone. "It is going to be a more difficult trek back to camp because we are carrying filled baskets."

Piero went in the lead, picking greens every so often. Maddia was less diligent, looking at the birds that flitted through the trees. She did not understand why, but birds were less common in winter. At this time of the year, more birds started appearing. She had asked Lartha about this, but the healer had only conjectures and no firm answer.

Nasha's low growl caused both Maddia and Piero to freeze. They saw immediately what had prompted the wolf's reaction. A group of aurochs had been grazing on a patch of first greens by the stream ahead of them. The three of them had gotten too near, and the males were on alert.

Male and female aurochs could be differentiated by their size and color. The males were larger, their horns were wider, and their color was darker. The young aurochs and females were a reddish brown. The older males were darker and often had a stripe down the middle of their back. The clan's hunters were proud to wear the striped skin of a male aurochs, both as a tribute to their bravery and to honor the creature.

For the most part, aurochs did not bother humans. When they saw humans coming, they would drift away. If the humans got too close, the males would form a defensive circle around the females and calves. If a human approached, one or more of the males would dig at the earth with its horns as a warning. If the human persisted, it might charge. An adult aurochs could gore or trample a human to death, even if the human had a weapon.

"Do not move, Piero," whispered Maddia. "Maybe the aurochs will go away."

Piero stood as still as a rock and said nothing. Maddia did the same, but Nasha could not control her instincts. She let out a growl and marched toward the enormous aurochs that was closest to them.

A pack of wolves is reluctant to challenge a mature aurochs, especially a male. They know it is wiser to look for a weak or injured animal. But Nasha was not hunting for food. She was protecting Maddia and Piero.

With the hair on her back raised, Nasha roamed back and forth in front of the aurochs. Neither wanted to attack, but neither would back off. Nasha's path in front of the aurochs got wider and wider, causing the aurochs to change position to keep an eye on her. In the meantime, the remaining animals clustered together. Some of them proceeded farther from the wolf and the two humans.

Nasha paced faster and faster in an ever-widening arc. She always stayed between the aurochs and the children, but the animal was ignoring them. It was totally focused on the wolf, a predator it knew well.

The wolf's behavior confused the aurochs. It was anticipating a direct assault and was perplexed by what the wolf was doing. No other wolves were in sight, so the aurochs was not as fearful as it had been initially. At the point where Nasha's path was farthest from the aurochs, it turned to look at the herd. The other aurochs had retired to a safe distance from the wolf. The male glanced at Nasha, who had come to a standstill, and with a snort, trotted off.

"Nasha, come here," whispered Maddia in a voice loud enough for the wolf to hear but not so loud that it would disturb the retreating aurochs. She and Piero were as immobile as they could be under the circumstances.

The wolf had a different idea. Little by little, she edged closer to the aurochs and continued pacing. It was clear that the wolf was trying to drive the group away from the children.

Maddia was terrified, and all she could think about was the aurochs turning and charging Nasha. Piero's mind was clouded with fear, but he was certain he did not want to be standing alone. He took a step closer to Maddia, then another. It seemed like forever, but by taking a dozen inconspicuous paces, he was beside her. With her free arm, Maddia pushed Piero behind her. Despite the urgency of the situation, they had not dropped the baskets they carried.

The aurochs, including the male that had threatened Nasha, wandered toward the canyon the children had just left. It was a sizable canyon, roughly a mile in length and half of a mile across at the widest point. The opening was relatively narrow, but there was plenty of room for the animals to get into the canyon. The sides of the canyon were too steep for the aurochs to climb, and the canyon ended in a cliff that was not quite straight up.

The children felt more at ease now that the aurochs had departed. They were beginning to understand that Nasha's maneuvers were intended to drive the aurochs farther from them.

"The aurochs are going into the canyon," observed Piero. With a relieved smile he went on to declare, "It is a good thing we gathered our greens before they got them."

A sudden noise startled the children. It was the hunters from the camp. Maddia turned quickly, and with her hands motioned for them to stop and be quiet. Everyone in the clan knew these signals. Responding to them was important for the survival of the clan, and children were taught the movements from their earliest years.

The hunters were not aware of what had taken place before, but they were pleased with what they saw. Nasha was driving the aurochs into the canyon. This would make hunting them considerably easier because the herd would be in a familiar location.

Nasha interrupted her pacing after the last of

the aurochs was in the canyon. She did not return to the humans, but lay down facing the canyon. Her ears were up, and as before, she never took her gaze from the animal that had threatened her. The aurochs, in contrast, was no longer concerned with the wolf and was grazing calmly.

Maddia turned to her father, who was leading the hunters today. She was going to explain what happened when Zibio interrupted.

"A large male aurochs has left the herd, which is going farther into the valley. Perhaps we can kill it without disturbing the others."

The hunters nodded in agreement. To their way of thinking, the hunt had become much easier and far less dangerous. Instead of stalking the aurochs, maybe for the better part of a day, before a single animal could be attacked, all they had to do was wait for the rest of them to drift away.

Only one hunter disagreed, the boy Griffo. He looked down, which was a traditional gesture in the clan made by those who wanted to address the others. The person would then wait until being recognized by the leader. Casting his eyes down was a cue for this, and Zibio turned to Griffo.

"You have something to say, Griffo?" Zibio's tone was considerate, as the clan had learned that listening, particularly to younger members, was necessary for building the sense of kinship that held the clan together.

"Hunting the aurochs that has left the herd might be simpler, but look at Nasha." Griffo pointed at the wolf. "She has driven the aurochs into the canyon, and while she is there, they will remain inside. Is there not a way we can keep the aurochs in the canyon?"

Chapter 17

Maddia and Piero understood what Griffo meant. The majority of the hunters did not. From their point of view, the most vital thing they could do was to kill an aurochs so the clan could eat for the next few days.

Ganni, Piero's older brother, walked over to Griffo. This shift of positions implied that he supported Griffo's idea. Zibio gave Ganni a chance to explain his thinking.

"Think of a hut," said Ganni. "The walls of the hut protect us, but they also prevent us from moving freely. Can we not make a wall to do the same thing to the aurochs in the valley?"

"Stupid boy," blurted Gortush. "It would take years to construct a hut to encircle the canyon."

The men looked at Gortush. His tone was disrespectful, and once more, his words were hurtful. Ganni looked angry, but as a boy, he could not confront Gortush. It was a good thing, because Ganni had the strength and quickness to defeat Gortush in a fair fight.

"We do not have to build a hut around the whole canyon," said Ganni. "All we have to do is block the mouth of the canyon. Let me show you."

Because he was a boy, Ganni's sudden words and actions were not considered to be insulting to the men who heard them. Gortush muttered to himself, but the hunters watched as the boy searched for enough sticks to demonstrate what he was suggesting.

"We begin by collecting sticks and logs. Then we stack them in this way." Ganni put several sticks on the ground, stacking them just so. It was like a game children played to see who could make the tallest pile.

"I understand," said Zibio. "We can make a wall. But will it be strong enough to hold the aurochs in? Will they not crash through?"

"Maybe they will not know how strong the wall is," said Maddia. "They might not want to try to knock it down. There are first greens in the canyon, and it will not be long before the grass starts growing. The spring will give them water. There is no reason for the aurochs to leave the canyon."

"Why are these children speaking out of turn," shouted Jartush. "Have they not been told their place?"

"Quiet, you fool," demanded Zibio. "You will frighten the aurochs."

Zibio was too late. Jartush's shrieking had agitated the aurochs. They became alert and milled around menacingly. Their behavior was an indication they might stampede at any time. As they became restless, Nasha rose from her lying position. She growled and once again strode back and forth across the mouth of the canyon. The aurochs stared at her for a moment and then turned and walked deeper into the canyon.

"Let us try what Ganni has proposed," ordered Zibio. "Maddia, bring your greens here. We have dried meat. We can eat the meat with your greens before we collect the sticks we will need. Piero, you take your greens to the camp. Ask the other men to join us. Tell them to hurry. We will need many hands to build the wall. And do not forget to return yourself to enjoy the hard work your brother has made for us."

Piero's chest swelled with pride. Zibio had treated him as a man, not a boy. He rushed toward the camp, and as he did, he heard the hunters tapping the ground softly with their spears. This act was a sign of encouragement that the men offered before undertaking a significant challenge.

The hunters got to work at once. The project was difficult because they could not cut trees or branches. They had no tools with them except their spears, and loud cutting noises might frighten the aurochs. Their sole recourse was to find fallen trees or branches. They worked noiselessly and brought their wood to the mouth of the canyon. They put down one log then another at a slight angle. The end of one log went on top of the end of another.

They alternated the ends of the logs so the wall was high enough to seem imposing to the aurochs.

While the men worked, the aurochs continued into the canyon. There was a sufficient distance between them and the humans so the aurochs did not feel fear. The wolf had retreated and was with the humans. The massive beasts saw little danger and proceeded to graze on the greens in the canyon.

Piero reappeared presently with more of the men. The women had also joined them, including Belia. The women brought grain cakes they had made for dinner that night. These cakes were made of crushed seeds and water, formed into flattened balls, and cooked on hot rocks beside the fire. Belia had advised bringing food, recognizing how hungry everyone would be as they created the wall.

The hunters explained to the new arrivals what they were doing, and then all of them got to work again. Slowly, the wall took shape and formed a barrier across the canyon.

While the older boys and men were transporting bulky logs, Maddia, Piero, and the women could gather only small logs and branches. They were not sure what to do with the smaller pieces of wood, so the women simply piled them against the wall. Belia surveyed the wall, considered the smaller lengths of wood, and had an idea. She tried weaving the smaller branches vertically between the logs. The pattern was similar to the arrangement of sticks Leeza had used to make baskets. After she and Maddia had done this with a dozen or so of the branches, they examined their work. The vertical lengths of wood increased the strength of the wall and made it look more substantial. Zibio, seeing what they were doing, walked over to them.

"That is very ingenious, my wife. The aurochs will probably not want to test the wall if they cannot see through it. They may believe that the canyon has closed in around them."

Maddia smiled at her father's words. Among the many things that she loved most about him was the way he recognized the efforts of others. He was willing to let them have their say, including the younger members of the clan, and he was quick to compliment them on their actions and ideas. She knew how pleased her mother was that her plan was received so well.

The wall was approaching completion, and the sun was low in the sky. The men and women who had built it were exhausted. Zibio ceased working and regarded the aurochs thoughtfully. He then turned to those around him and said wryly, "We have not been as clever as we should have been. The aurochs are in the valley, but we have little for our evening meal. Piero's greens and a few seed cakes are not enough to sustain us. Do you think we can lure an aurochs to where we can kill it?"

Those who heard what he said spoke among themselves with uncertainly and a touch of apprehension because none of them had ever tried to coax an aurochs closer. They hunted by surprise, hoping for a sudden kill before the aurochs was aware of what was happening.

"Nasha and I can try to draw an aurochs toward the mouth of the canyon," suggested Maddia. A team of hunters can hide by the spring and strike when it gets within range."

Belia, who overheard Maddia's words, argued with motherly logic. "It is too dangerous for you, daughter. An experienced hunter should do it."

"Nasha will not obey or protect a hunter. Her loyalty is to me. I am the only person who can work with her to attract the aurochs. Please let us try."

Belia persisted with her objections, but Zibio decided the proposal was worth trying. He and some of the men, including the boy Griffo, would form the hunting party. They walked quietly through the part of the wall that was not yet completed. The hunters hid behind a rocky outcropping beside the waterfall. The mist of the falling water would help to conceal them, and the sound of the tumbling water prevented the aurochs from hearing them.

When the hunters were in place, Zibio waved to Maddia. She took a deep breath and patted her thigh so Nasha would see the gesture. The wolf understood that Maddia wanted her to stay close. The two of them trooped into the canyon where they could be seen by the aurochs.

As had happened before, the largest male walked toward them. He snorted, pawed the ground, and dug up clods of earth with his horns. Nasha growled and set her ears back, but she never left Maddia.

The aurochs strode forward, and Maddia shifted backward. She made a small noise under her breath and Nasha came to her immediately. The aurochs was turning to reunite with the herd when Maddia slapped her thigh, getting the animal's attention. Sensing a threat, the aurochs took several more steps, bellowing and waving its horns menacingly. It was too distant for the hunters to attack without disturbing the rest of the animals.

Nasha could take no more of the threats from the aurochs. She strode forward before Maddia could whisper a command to bring her back. It was too late, and the aurochs began to charge. Maddia called out to Nasha. She turned and darted toward the opening in the wall. Nasha hesitated protectively before joining Maddia. The aurochs continued onward but balked as it came to the wall, puzzled by an impediment it did not remember or recognize.

The hunters hiding by the outcropping attacked together on Zibio's signal. Swiftly and quietly, they ran toward the aurochs. Zibio drove his spear into the animal's ribs just behind the front leg, causing a mortal wound that would ultimately kill the aurochs. He bounded away quickly as the aurochs turned, and the hunters struck with their weapons. Despite being mortally injured, the aurochs could inflict substantial harm. The animal bellowed and thrashed its head, but the spears had done their work. It staggered and swayed clumsily before collapsing to the ground.

The other aurochs had watched for a moment, but their instincts soon took over. They milled about and then trotted toward the far end of the canyon. On the way they passed a bend in the canyon, after which they could not see the humans or the wolf. No danger was apparent, so they lessened their pace before coming to a stop. After a time of cautious waiting, the aurochs returned to grazing as if nothing had happened.

The men who had remained beyond the wall now teamed up with the hunters. They were prepared to strike if the aurochs had only been wounded, but it did not stir. The aurochs was dead, and the clan would eat well that night. Silently, the hunters honored the tradition of thanking the aurochs for offering its life that they and their families might have nourishment.

The work was not yet complete. The most critical thing to be done was to transport the aurochs beyond the wall. This was difficult because the carcass weighed so much. Normally, the hunters would hack the aurochs into pieces with stone cutting tools, but that would take too long. They would have to get the beast through the gap and then restore the logs to the wall.

There was no easy way to drag the beast. The eight strongest hunters, four on each side, pulled the aurochs by its horns. Two others pushed from behind. It was exhausting work, but they eventually got the animal on the outside of the fence.

Something curious occurred as the aurochs was being dragged. Two of the hunters had put their spears down, and when the aurochs was drawn over them, it moved more easily than when it was hauled on the ground. Zibio noted this and thought he should discuss it with Fong the next time they were together.

The hunters commenced at once to use their cutting tools on the aurochs. They skinned the animal and then cut the meat into hunks that could be borne easily. Two of the men would use the skin to transport some of the meat to the camp. The skin would then be awarded to one of hunters. Nasha was given a portion of flesh, which she took aside and chewed with enthusiasm. The hunters, the women, and the children continued building the wall across the canyon. They worked with haste because it would be dark in a little while, and they wanted to get to camp while there was sufficient light to travel safely.

The wall was at last completed. It was the height of a man's shoulder and looked substantial. The clan hoped that the aurochs would be intimidated by the unfamiliar sight and would not try to knock it down. A single aurochs could undoubtedly damage the wall, and the herd could crash through it effortlessly.

"That is all the meat we can carry," said Zibio. "It is more than enough for a feast tonight. We can put the leftover meat on spears and pick it up tomorrow."

Putting the meat on spears was a simple but effective idea that his wife's sister, Leeza, had conceived. She had discovered that a large piece of meat could be suspended on spears. Three hunters put the butts of their spears on the ground with the points facing upward. Other hunters would lift the meat up and impale it on the spear points. With a little adjusting, the three spears could support the meat, and it would not topple over easily. For many of the people in the clan, seeing the meat suspended this way was verging on magical. The meat seemed to float in the air, and because three spears were used, it was very stable. Elevating the meat was the perfect way to keep it from smaller animals. A bear or lion could reach the meat, of course, but wolves and foxes could not.

Each member of the clan carried some of the meat to the camp. As they walked, they had animated conversations and reviewed what had transpired that day, especially the extraordinary things that Maddia, Nasha, and Piero had accomplished. They wondered if the aurochs would spend the night in the valley, and they could not wait to bring their friends to see the wall they had built.

Chapter 18

The clan had a feast to celebrate the occasion. The meat from the aurochs was roasted in a blazing fire, and more seed cakes were cooked on stones beside the flames. The camp was filled with delicious aromas, and those who were involved told the story of what happened at the canyon. Checo, the blind poet, listened attentively. It would be his job to retell the narrative for years to come, embellishing it with the passage of time.

When the meat was ready, it was shared among the entire clan, not only those who had participated in the events of the day. Baratho had instituted this practice when he assumed leadership of the clan. A few grumbled about this distribution, most notably Gortush, but it was clear that the sharing of the food had made the clan strong. There were many healthy children, and the older people were living longer while contributing to the clan's well being.

After they had eaten, Baratho rapped his staff

on a log. When the group became silent, he said, "Momentous things took place today. I am unclear about what they will mean to us in the time to come, but I feel that the whole clan should see what has been accomplished. Tomorrow, I urge the clan as a group, including the old ones and children, to visit the spring and see the wall and the aurochs. We shall then discuss what should occur next. I want all of you to sleep well so that we will be fresh tomorrow."

Baratho looked at Lartha, who nodded back at him. It was evident that he had consulted with her before making this decision. She turned from the fire and walked toward her shelter, and the rest of the clan went their own ways shortly.

On the following morning, the entire camp prepared for the trek to the canyon. It was infrequent when everyone was absent from camp at the same time. This only happened when the clan traveled from one region to another. There were many risks associated with leaving a camp unguarded, but Baratho was of the opinion that the whole clan should see the wall and the aurochs. Besides, the clan's most valuable asset, its members, would all be together.

The jaunt to the canyon was slow but uneventful. The young children insisted on frolicking, and the old people took their time, enjoying a rare excursion out of the camp. Maddia stayed with her mother, who tried unsuccessfully to have Lakus remain nearby. The boy lagged behind with Nasha, who delighted in the affection he showed her and the opportunity to chase sticks he threw.

"You are quiet, Maddia," said Belia. "What is worrying you?"

"What if the wall has fallen down and the aurochs are gone? Our trip will have been wasted, and we will have left the camp unguarded. The clan will blame Baratho. I will feel responsible because Piero and I wandered into the group of aurochs."

Belia put her arm around Maddia and said confidently, "Baratho would not have brought us here if he did not think it was important. I believe he discussed the situation with Lartha, and she must have seen the value of this journey. She understands many things that we cannot. Besides, it is a gorgeous morning. The children are having a wonderful time, and the old ones are behaving as if they were youthful again."

As the clan came close to the canyon, those who had not seen the wall before gasped. Even those who had built the wall were in awe. It was the largest structure the clan had made, and in the light of day, the accomplishment was more imposing than it had appeared the night before. The barrier was intact, and the aurochs were grazing peacefully within the canyon.

Leeza guided Checo to the wall. He placed his hands on it, and the two of them sidled along it for a short distance. Checo touched the wall as they walked, marveling at its size and construction.

"Building the wall was a remarkable effort. I

wonder if humans anywhere else have made structures like this?" Checo was clearly inspired by what he was feeling. "And you say that the aurochs are trapped in the canyon beyond the wall?"

"Yes," answered Leeza, "and they seem to have no interest in leaving. There is plenty of food and water for them, and they have grazed in this canyon before."

"Griffo's idea was indeed worthy," said Baratho. He spoke so that everyone could hear yet softly enough to avoid disturbing the aurochs. "To him will go the skin of the aurochs that was killed yesterday."

The boy Griffo was pleased but silent. From the look on his face, it was evident that he felt well-deserved pride, but it was clouded by sadness. He was the youngest hunter ever to earn a skin, yet his parents, who had died when he was an infant, were not present to share in his success. He did not stand alone, for Leeza, Ganni, and Piero had come to his side. Leeza had taken Griffo into her family upon the passing of his mother and father, even though her husband had also died and she had two small children.

Maddia stared fondly at Griffo, and he glanced back at her briefly, embarrassed by the attention he was receiving. Their gaze was broken by Katia, who jabbed Maddia in the ribs with her elbow. Maddia giggled, knowing that her fondness for Griffo was hardly a secret.

Acting as if he had played a role in capturing the

aurochs, Jartush made a pronouncement. "By slaying these aurochs, we can eat for days as never before. What we do not consume now we can trade for golden stones. Our clan will be the envy of the others."

A faint voice came from behind the men. "But why do we have to kill the whole herd?" whispered Piero. "We cannot eat all of them, and we have no use for golden stones. Can we not keep the aurochs alive for another time?"

"The small one is practical," responded Lartha, looking at Piero with admiration. "There is food for the aurochs in the canyon. The stream that runs through it brings water in every season. The steep walls will provide shelter when the weather becomes harsh. The aurochs will be healthy and available for our use if they stay in the canyon."

"They will consume all the grass, they will die, and we will have not gained anything," grumbled Gortush. "We should feast on them and trade what is left for golden stones." He glared at Piero, who slid behind his brother, Ganni.

"We can bring the aurochs food if they exhaust the grass in the valley, but that will not usually be necessary." Baratho's statement was muted on purpose so those with him would have to strain to hear. He had discovered that the big noises made by Gortush did little to make his words believable. Instead, Baratho spoke in a way that encouraged listening and thinking.

"Think of a fire," argued Baratho. "When the fire

burns low, we bring it more wood. The fire grows hotter. We can perform a similar action with the aurochs. If the grass is eaten, we will bring more. There is plenty of grass beside the river for us to harvest. It is work that women and children can do while the men are hunting bison."

And so it was that the clan kept the aurochs in the canyon as Piero had suggested. Feeling an attachment to the animals, Piero became their overseer and ensured that they had an ample supply of food.

The grass in the canyon was usually sufficient for the aurochs. From time to time, the aurochs consumed the grass at the far end of the canyon and looked for forage closer to the barrier the clan had built. Piero and his helpers whose duty was to feed the aurochs gathered grass in baskets and put it inside the enclosure. Some of the grass had recently grown, but much of it was from the past summer and retained its seeds.

Several days after putting grass in the enclosure, Piero noticed something. Many young plants grew from where the grass had been placed. Piero thought no more about it, and the aurochs quickly ate the grass. New sprouts appeared the next time that Piero put grass in the enclosure for the aurochs.

Piero told Tulio what occurred. His cousin said that new plants often sprang up where other plants of the same kind had been. He advised an experiment of sorts. They would put some of the grass on the outside of the stockade and the rest on the inside to see what happened.

Within three or four days, grass shoots poked through the soil where Piero had put the seeds. Inside the enclosure, the aurochs ate the fresh grass as well as the old grass. Beyond the enclosure, the grass was taller. Piero told Tulio what happened, and the two boys inspected the grass that Piero had put down.

"I thought maybe the old grass came to life again," said Piero, "but look. The old grass is still here. The sprouts only appeared where the seeds were."

"We should show Lartha what you found. I think your discovery might be beneficial for the clan."

The two boys made their way to camp and described to Lartha what had happened. They were surprised that she did not want to go and see the grass that had grown from the seeds. She asked that they bring seeds to her, and they would see if they grew in another place.

Piero was visibly disappointed in her response. He wanted Lartha to see the plants that were already growing. Tulio made him feel better when he explained what Lartha was probably thinking. "She respects your judgment and does not doubt that your thinking is correct. She is giving you a chance to prove your idea with another test."

On the following dawn, Piero and Tulio went to the spot where Piero usually found the grass to feed the aurochs. Rather than collecting the grass indiscriminately, they picked the stems with seeds attached. They brought the seeds to Lartha, and the three of them selected an area for the trial. Lartha urged them to identify a plot in the vicinity of her shelter that was similar to where the seeds had done well before. They chose a patch of loose soil by the stream that was usually in the sun. The ground was a little wet, like the ground by the aurochs where the seeds had grown before.

Each day, Piero and Tulio came back to check the seeds. On the fourth day, the seeds had sprouted. They pointed this out to Lartha, who was just as excited as the boys.

"I am undecided about what is more amazing," she said to Piero, "your realizing that seeds could be made to grow plants wherever we want, or the failure of humans to have come to this conclusion before. In all my years, I did not make the connection between seeds and plants."

The grass grew well where the boys had planted the seeds. Lartha invited Baratho and the clan elders to see what the boys had done. She allowed the boys to explain how they had made the discovery, wanting them to get credit for what they had done.

"It seems so simple, once you think it over," said Baratho. "Plants make seeds, and from seeds come young plants. Piero and Tulio used the seed from a single kind of grass. When they planted the seeds, the same type of grass sprouted."

Lartha added, "Each plant must have its own seed. If we can find the seeds of the most useful plants, we can grow them where we choose.

Gathering will be easier because our food plants will be closer to camp. And to think, all of this came of Piero's willingness to feed the aurochs."

Chapter 19

By late in her second summer, Nasha was fully grown. She was a long-legged gray wolf who had incredible strength but a good-natured demeanor. Nasha wandered the camp freely when she wanted, and she was welcome by every family. The majority of the time, however, she was not far from Maddia's side.

One of Maddia's duties was to accompany the women when they left camp to find food. Nasha always went with her. The search for food started in the morning and was usually finished by the middle of the afternoon, at which time the women would return to camp and prepare the food. A portion of it would be used for the evening meal, and whatever was left would be set aside for use at another time.

A hunter was usually assigned to go with the women to guard them, often joined by several of the bigger boys. During the time the women were out, hunters would visit them, both to ensure their protection and to give them a break from their labor.

On this day, the women would be picking seeds from plants that were in a large meadow. The meadow had been Piero's idea. Based on his observation that plants flourished where seeds had been scattered for the aurochs in the canyon, Piero had tried scattering them in a variety of places. Sometimes they did not grow, but in certain areas, the seeds sprouted into plants that produced seeds in greater abundance than did wild plants. This meadow was one of the locations where the seeds did well.

The women cut the plants just above the ground with a stone tool and put them in baskets. In the past, the women were interested in just the seeds because this was the part of the plant that the clan ate. After the aurochs had been trapped in the canyon, Belia advised that they should harvest leaves and stems as well as seeds. Back at the camp, the women removed the seeds, and the rest of the plant was fed to the aurochs.

Katia and Maddia were at the edge of the meadow cutting plants. Nasha relaxed, keeping a watchful eye on the girls. Periodically, she would rise, stretch, and pace to another location, sniffing the air and inspecting the surroundings as she did.

A flock of birds that had been roosting in a thicket of trees took flight. Nasha became uneasy and trotted to the girls. She positioned herself in front of Maddia and kept her eyes on the woods from which the birds had flown.

"Silly Nasha," said Maddia, "it was only some birds. Why would a big, strong wolf be afraid of birds?"

Normally, Maddia's soft words would have drawn Nasha to her side for a hug around her neck, but this time Nasha was transfixed, staring at the forest. A low growl rolled from her throat, and the hairs down the center of her back rose up.

"What is it, Nasha?" asked Maddia, looking at the trees. She had learned that Nasha's senses were sharper than hers, and if Nasha perceived danger, something had caused it.

Katia also knew of Nasha's alertness, and she dropped the plants she held and walked over to Maddia. The two of them scanned the trees and finally saw what had triggered Nasha's growl. Standing at the edge of the woods was a white wolf.

It was unusual to see a lone wolf, particularly this close to a group of humans. Wolves usually hunted and traveled in a pack, so Maddia and Katia looked for other wolves. They saw none, and Nasha had not taken her eyes from the white wolf, which was an indication that there were no others nearby.

Wolf packs are led by a dominant animal, which is usually a male. Another wolf may occasionally raise a challenge, and a fight will ensue. It is quick and violent, with the current leader usually winning. The loser of the confrontation may remain with the pack in a subservient role or withdraw from the pack. Wolves that are separated from a pack rarely make it on their own, and they are not typically welcome in another pack.

A loud yell from behind them startled the girls, Nasha, and the white wolf. It was Tulio, Maddia's older brother. Armed with a spear, he hurried to the girls. As he did, the white wolf bounded away.

Unexpectedly, Nasha took off in the direction of the wolf. Maddia's shout had no effect on her, and Nasha ran to where the white wolf had been. Arriving at the spot, she turned in a circle, sniffing vigorously all the while. She caught the white wolf's scent, tracked it, and then stopped. The white wolf was between two trees, motionless but staring at her intently.

Maddia was terrified, anxious about what would happen. She dared not move for fear of threatening the white wolf, which might attack Nasha or them. Tulio opened his mouth to make a comment, but Maddia hushed him politely.

The two wolves walked toward one another until they were together. They smelled each other curiously and circled around. Nasha halted, as did the white wolf, and they stood nose to nose. Nasha's tail wagged, slowly at first, and then more happily. The white wolf behaved in a similar way. In an instant, they were nudging each other, nipping gently, and pawing playfully.

Tulio whispered quietly, "Do they recognize each other? I have seen wolves do this before, but only with other animals from the same pack."

"How could she know the white wolf?" wondered Katia. "Nasha has not been away from you, has she?"

"I have no idea how," answered Maddia, "but Nasha seems to remember the white wolf. Nasha has not spent any time by herself without me, and I have not seen this wolf before." She hesitated and then asked, "Could it be that the white wolf was from Nasha's pack when she was a pup?"

A worrisome thought came to Maddia, one she had tried to bury ever since the day long ago when Nasha had heard the howls of far-away wolves. She was just a pup then, but what would happen if Nasha came upon a pack of wolves now? Maddia had seen Nasha respond when she heard the songs of wolves. She would pace, put her ears back, and howl herself, but she never went far from Maddia. Looking at Nasha, Maddia was worried she might lose her.

"Come, Nasha," said Maddia in a commanding voice. She advanced toward the wolves and said it one more time.

Immediately, Nasha obeyed the command. As usual, she trotted toward Maddia. Taking a dozen steps, she looked behind her. The white wolf had not stirred, so Nasha returned to him, put her head on his shoulder for a moment, and then returned to Maddia. The white wolf trailed behind her but waited at a distance of fifty yards or so while Nasha strolled to Maddia.

From where she was, Maddia could see that the

white wolf was a male, a little smaller than Nasha, and much thinner. He studied the four of them but would come no closer.

Nasha scampered to the white wolf and then to Maddia. She was encouraging him to join them, but he would not budge. Maddia was unsure about what to do and felt her concern rising.

"Let us go," said Tulio. "The white wolf may be by himself, but he is still a threat."

Nasha looked at Maddia and whimpered. Although Maddia knew that Tulio was well intentioned, she felt no fear of the white wolf. In addition, if the white wolf had posed any danger to Nasha, she would not behave this way.

"You two walk over to the others," said Maddia. "I am going to stay here with Nasha and see what the white wolf does. I have a cutting stone and Nasha to defend myself."

"That is foolish," argued Tulio. "Not every wolf is like Nasha."

"You are right, but I feel I must try. Look how thin the wolf is. Listen to Nasha. I cannot simply abandon him."

"Do what Tulio suggests," begged Katia. "If the white wolf attacks, we could not rescue you."

"I hear what you are saying, but something is telling me to trust the white wolf. It is comparable to the feeling I had on the day I first saw Nasha. Please, give me a chance. Let me see what the white wolf does."

Tulio turned to Nasha and said sincerely, "Take

care of my sister. Let her come to no harm." He put his hand on Maddia's head as if to share his strength and then turned to Katia. "Nasha will protect Maddia. Let us go. We can watch from a distance."

As the two of them retreated, Maddia pulled dried meat and a seed cake out of her tunic. She sat on the ground and said to Nasha, "Bring him to me." Nasha whimpered happily and raced to the wolf.

Maddia threw a piece of meat as far as she could in front of her. She hoped Nasha would not gobble it if she did manage to bring the white wolf near.

With the two humans leaving and the third sitting on the ground, the white wolf was a little more comfortable. He frolicked with Nasha and seemed to pay no attention as she neared the seated human.

When the two of them got to within ten paces of Maddia, the white wolf drew up. Nasha trudged back and forth between them, whimpering. The white wolf took a few more steps but was reluctant to come any closer. Nasha ceased her pacing as she passed the meat Maddia had put on the ground and snatched it.

"Nasha, that's not for you," whispered Maddia. Her heart sank as she saw her plan to attract the wolf fall apart.

Nasha, to Maddia's relief, did not consume the meat. She walked over to the white wolf and dropped it in front of him. Maddia had seen Nasha do this before with sticks when she wanted to play, and a smile crept into her face. *What a thoughtful wolf she was.*

The white wolf investigated the meat and then picked it up eagerly. He chewed it vigorously before devouring it and looked at Nasha as if he wanted more.

Maddia threw another scrap of meat in front of her, and Nasha immediately ran to it. Instinctively, the white wolf did the same, forgetting the presence of the human. When he came up to the meat, he paused and looked at Nasha as if offering her an opportunity to eat it. Her hesitation was ample encouragement, and he gobbled it quickly.

Now that the white wolf was almost upon her, Maddia could see how gaunt it was. He was a handsome animal, but his coat was sparse, and his ribs showed through his skin. He looked at Maddia cautiously, but she perceived no threat.

Speaking softly, Maddia urged the white wolf forward and held another bit of meat where he could reach it comfortably. As she did, Nasha bumped against her affectionately, glancing often at the white wolf. It drew close and took the meat readily from Maddia's hand. Drifting back, it chewed and swallowed the meat.

Maddia repeated the process with bits of meat and pieces of seed cake. Each time, she let the wolf sniff her hand before allowing him to have the treat. He pushed his cold nose against her, and on one of the exchanges, he licked her hand.

The interaction between Maddia and the wolf was observed by Tulio, Katia, and their companions. They were silent but awe-struck at what was happening. Maddia's raising Nasha had become a legend among the clan members, but because she was a pup, there was more understanding of its possibility. For Maddia to have tamed a wild wolf, however, was beyond anything they could imagine.

After feeding the white wolf the food she had, Maddia remained seated. Nasha nudged her several times, demanding to be petted. She then plopped down beside Maddia and rolled on her back. Maddia stroked Nasha's belly before the wolf turned onto her side. The white wolf lay down in front of Maddia with his paws almost touching Nasha. It sighed deeply and shut its eyes, grateful for the presence of other animals, even if one of them was a human. Laying its head between its outstretched legs, the white wolf began to doze.

Chapter 20

The white wolf slept, and Maddia kept as still as she could, not wanting to disturb him. Nasha was very much awake, acting as a guard for Maddia and the sleeping wolf. Tulio, Katia, and the others returned to their work gathering seeds. They were so far from Maddia and the wolves that they could discuss the matter quietly without waking the white wolf.

A party of children from the camp, led by Lartha, joined the workers, laughing and shouting as they advanced. Hearing the voices, the white wolf woke with a start. He jumped to his feet and placed himself defensively between the approaching humans and Maddia. Nasha cocked her hears, but being more familiar with humans, she did not feel threatened.

Uttering a low growl, the white wolf turned to look at Nasha. Her relaxed attitude had the effect of calming him slightly, and he became quiet.

Nonetheless, he paced warily, seeming unsure of the humans standing in the distance.

"They are friends," said Maddia soothingly. She unhurriedly changed her position from sitting to kneeling on all fours. "They will not hurt us."

Nasha got up and leaned against Maddia's leg. Seeing this, the white wolf wiggled his body between Maddia and Nasha. This typical wolf behavior is evidence of playful jealousy, and the three of them cuddled fondly.

Maddia rose and continued to stroke both wolves patiently. She made a hand signal telling Nasha to sit. Recognizing the movement, Nasha obediently discontinued her playing and sat down. Seeing this, the white wolf sat also, shifting his gaze between Nasha and Maddia.

Giving Nasha another hand gesture to stay, Maddia withdrew from the wolves and headed in the direction of Tulio and Katia. She stopped, turned toward the wolves, and motioned again. The white wolf tilted his head and examined Maddia quizzically, and then he looked back at Nasha. Seeing that she was sitting, he did the same. Maddia continued to edge closer to Tulio and Katia.

"You cannot bring the white wolf to our camp," whispered Tulio as soon as Maddia could hear him. "You do not know what he will do with unfamiliar people around. I am troubled about what the rest of the clan will do."

"Tulio is making a lot of sense," said Katia. "Those with us are already making it clear that they are not comfortable with the white wolf."

"I cannot leave him," pleaded Maddia. "He might track us to the camp, or he might not hunt successfully. He is a young wolf who is alone. He will not survive. Help me decide what I should do."

The three of them glanced at the wolves. They continued to sit, though the white wolf looked anxiously between Nasha and Maddia.

"Look how he obeys you despite not having been with you before today. How can that be?" wondered Katia.

"It is how wolves are," whispered a voice from behind them. Lartha had silently withdrawn from the group of small children and was with Tulio.

"Wolves are like us in many ways. They learn from one another, especially when there is uncertainty. The white wolf trusts Maddia and Nasha. From afar, I saw how he acted with you." Lartha spoke softly and looked at Maddia. "What do you want to do now?"

"I am at a loss about what to do," answered Maddia. "I do not want to abandon the white wolf, but I am not sure that he should come to the camp. The clan will be uneasy, and so might the wolf."

"Let us see how he does with other humans," advised Lartha. "Call the wolves to us and we will see how he acts."

Waving her hand in a way with which Nasha was familiar, Maddia said, "Come, Nasha." She added hopefully, "And bring the white wolf."

Nasha paced toward Maddia but halted suddenly.

She turned and looked at the white wolf, expecting him to be behind her, but he was not. Nasha returned and circled him twice. She rubbed her head under his jaw and poked him with her nose. She turned toward Maddia, and the white wolf came behind her.

As the wolves advanced, Tulio placed himself in front of Katia and Lartha to shield them from a possible attack. He was wary of the white wolf, and he dearly loved his sister. He attempted to protect Maddia, but she put her arm in front of him.

"Let the wolves come to me," said Maddia. "We have to be trusting."

Nasha ran up to Maddia, who knelt down to hug the gray wolf's neck. The white wolf waited several feet away, whimpering.

"Come, Albo," said Maddia. She addressed the wolf using the clan's name for the wind that brought the snow.

The white wolf came timidly toward Maddia, who extended her hand and scratched him behind the ears. As she did, the wolf snuggled into her chest and whimpered adoringly. Nasha pushed her head into Maddia's hands and nibbled playfully at the white wolf's neck.

Maddia arose and motioned to Nasha, who sat immediately. Seeing her do this, Albo sat beside her.

Lartha reached inside her tunic and brought out some dried meat. She took a step, paused, and then took another. Albo began to rise, but seeing that Nasha was sitting, he backed down again. Lartha extended her hand with a piece of meat toward the white wolf. He looked at Nasha and Maddia for assurance. Then he delicately took the meat from Lartha's hand. He chewed the meat cautiously before consuming it, all the while looking at Lartha.

"You are a fine wolf, Albo," whispered Lartha, and she offered both animals another strip of meat. She did this several times, allowing Albo to smell her hand as she did.

"This does not solve our problem," suggested Lartha, "but I believe the white wolf can be trusted, at least with us. I still do not think we can take him to the camp. Too many things can go wrong. We should find another place."

"Would the cave near the aurochs work?" said Tulio. He lowered his hand toward the white wolf, which studied it cautiously. Albo then bumped Tulio's hand with his nose, surprising the others because he thus far had been so shy. Tulio turned his hand over and unfolded his fingers, showing a slice of dried meat, which Albo took without hesitation.

"Our hunter's heart has obviously warmed to the white wolf," commented Lartha. She smiled at Tulio, who was somewhat embarrassed. "But Tulio's idea is worth considering. Hiding in the cave will give Albo a chance to get used to new people."

The four of them discussed what to do. Lartha, Tulio, Maddia, and the wolves would make their way to the cave. Katia would go to camp and tell Zibio and Belia where the three of them and the wolves would be waiting. Lartha repeated a list of supplies that would let the three of them stay in the cave comfortably. Katia memorized the list and promised not to tell anyone else about the plan.

"It is important that only Zibio and Belia know where we are," insisted Lartha. "There are those in the camp who might want to harm Albo. Ask Zibio and Belia to keep our location a secret, and one of them should bring the supplies." Katia nodded and joined the gatherers, who had completed their work and were heading to camp.

The three of them and Nasha walked toward the cave where they would pass the coming days. Surprisingly, Albo joined them without encouragement, acting as if Nasha and the humans were his pack. Tulio, who seemed to have an endless stockpile of dried meat and seed cake, let the wolves have a treat every now and then.

"Your brother must have a magic tunic. Every time he reaches into it, he retrieves more food." Lartha grinned at the young hunter.

"Mother says Tulio has been a devoted eater for all of his days," commented Maddia. "As a child, he usually carried the amount of food necessary to make the winter journey." She referred to the odyssey the clan made in the past between their summer and winter homes.

Laughing at their words, Tulio leaned down and inadvertently petted Albo in the way he had often stroked Nasha. The white wolf, rather than shrinking away, drew closer to the boy.

"Our new wolf makes friends easily," said Lartha. "That is a hopeful sign." She stared into the distance and said out loud, "It is as if he were a docga."

Tulio and Maddia nodded in agreement. In their clan and other clans from the same tradition, a docga was a mysterious stranger who came to humans in a time of troubles. A docga would guide a clan through a difficult situation, bring a desperately needed gift, or resolve a dispute in an equitable way. The docga might continue living with the clan or disappear just as mysteriously as he or she had appeared.

"I never thought of Nasha in that way," said Maddia, "but you are right, as always, Lartha. Nasha brought us a matchless gift by driving the aurochs into the canyon. Perhaps Albo will bring us a similar gift."

They arrived at the cave shortly and drank from the spring before going inside. While the humans took it easy, the two wolves paced in front of the wall of wood that kept the aurochs confined. Although they could not see the aurochs, they recognized their scent.

Hearing an unfamiliar sound, the two wolves ceased their pacing. They bounded to the mouth of the cave and stood defensively in front of the humans. In the distance, Zibio marched toward the cave bearing supplies wrapped in an animal skin. Before getting to them, Zibio called Maddia's name.

Lartha reacted quickly. "Tulio, have Zibio wait before coming to the cave. We will summon him when we are ready. Maddia, call the wolves to you.

I am uneasy about how Albo will respond to an unfamiliar human."

Maddia had Nasha and Albo sit in the opening of the cave. She placed herself in front of them, keeping a hand on each wolf. Lartha waved, and Zibio walked toward them with Tulio at his side. Understanding the situation, he approached slowly.

Albo watched the stranger draw closer. The wolf did not panic, but he appeared tense. Maddia murmured to him and made sure Nasha did not run to greet Zibio.

Tulio had taken the supplies from Zibio, and he put them in a corner away from the wolves. Maddia told him to come closer to her and asked her father to follow him. It took a while, but eventually Tulio was standing next to Albo, and Zibio was not much farther away. The wolf did not seem bothered, so Maddia had the two of them sit down. Patting the ground, Maddia signaled for Nasha to lie down, and Albo lay down beside her.

"I see you have enchanted a second wolf, daughter. Your kindness is admirable, but another wolf might be troubling for the clan." Zibio chose his words thoughtfully, considering the requirements of the clan, Maddia, and the wolf.

"Maddia understands that the white wolf poses challenges for us. He might not want to be with us after he has been fed," said Lartha. "In any case, Albo—that is the name Maddia selected for him—is not a pup. His needs will be different from Nasha's in many ways."

"What are you thinking?" asked Zibio. "Because you requested food and such, I am assuming that Maddia and the wolves plan to spend some time here."

"I will keep her company," said Tulio. "She cannot be left undefended."

Zibio nodded at his son, gratified that he was being so supportive of his sister and the white wolf. "You may stay with her. I suspect that Lakus will want to join you, and if that is his decision, your mother and I will spend time with all of you. Let me go to camp and tell Lakus and your mother."

"I am sorry to make things difficult for you." Maddia was apologetic, believing that her parents' decision would be met with disapproval by at least some of the clan.

Zibio got up carefully in order to avoid disturbing the two wolves. Albo looked at him inquisitively, but he did not get up. Being more accustomed to the ways of humans, Nasha continued to lie where she was.

On his way out of the cave, Zibio saw a figure on the path in the distance. He hurried his pace, hoping to prevent whoever it was from reaching the cave and discovering the white wolf. As he did so, his heart sank. It was Baratho, the last person he wanted to see.

When he was close enough, Baratho could see the look of dismay on Zibio's face, and he tried to reassure him. "It is fine, Zibio. I heard rumors of the white wolf. Maddia's plan to keep it a secret did not account for the excitement of the other children. They showed up in camp with an amazing tale. When I saw you leaving camp with a bundle, I concluded that you had become part of the plan."

At a loss for words, Zibio just stood there and then mumbled, "Thank you, Baratho. My daughter means well, but she sometimes does not consider how her actions will affect the clan. Bringing another wolf to our camp might be dangerous, and I can understand why people might be troubled."

Baratho smiled and said, "You will be delighted to hear that once the children told the story, almost everyone in the camp wanted to see the white wolf. Nasha plays such an important role in our clan that another wolf would be welcome."

"I hope this comes to pass, Baratho. I am greatly relieved. My principal concern was for the others in the clan. Their support will make the job of taming Albo easier," said Zibio.

"So, the wolf has a name already," commented Baratho. "I have not seen the wolf, but from what the children said, it is the perfect name."

As they walked toward the camp, Zibio explained what they planned to do. Baratho suggested that each day, a small number of other clan members might visit the cave. The plan worked well, and over time, Albo grew accustomed to humans.

Because he was not exposed as a pup to humans, Albo did not feel as comfortable with them as did Nasha. He was at his best with Nasha, Maddia, and her family. While Nasha would frolic with the children of the clan, Albo was more reserved. He was very protective of the clan, however, and on most nights, he would circle through the camp several times before falling asleep outside Maddia's shelter in a hole he had dug under a log. Nasha periodically accompanied him on these rounds, but she inevitably went into the shelter to sleep beside Maddia.

Chapter 21

As the clan's healer, Lartha had a responsibility that was of spiritual and practical importance. She had to track the turning of the seasons by observing the transition of the sun.

The tradition of tracking the sun's progress across the sky stretched back beyond memory to the time when all humans were nomadic and wandered from place to place. Anticipating the seasons helped the leader decide when to relocate and where they should go. When winter was near, the clan had to seek an area with better weather and more game. In the warmer times of the year, the clan had to follow the migrating animals and identify when plants would produce edible roots, fruit, or seeds.

There was also a superstitious reason that humans tracked the passage of the sun. As the days got shorter, ancient people came to believe that the sun might set and never rise again. This would mean

eternal darkness and the cessation of their existence, so many ceremonies were undertaken on the
shortest day to entreat the sun to remain in the sky.

Because the clan had been in this valley for
more than a year, Lartha knew where the sun would
set on the shortest day. She had designated the spot
with two stakes and a circle of stones the previous
year. This year, she had a request of Baratho. On a
day late in the fall, she met with him to discuss her
proposition.

"In order to petition the sun to return and to celebrate the clan's new home, I would like us to raise a
standing stone. Is this something you would consider?" Lartha was confident that Baratho would
agree to her request, but she showed him the respect
he deserved by choosing her words deliberately.

"Your idea pleases me." Baratho beamed as he
responded to her request, and he could not wait to
share it. "Let us spread the news."

Baratho waved his arms and addressed those
who were around him in the camp. He spoke to
them with a joyful tone.

"As you are aware, many of the village clans have
a custom of erecting great stones. Lartha has proposed that we do this for the ceremony to honor
the sun on the shortest day. I think her proposal is
more than fitting. The stone monument will be our
way of honoring the sun and will represent our possible settlement here. Please tell your friends this
wonderful news."

The entire clan had soon been told of the monumental stone. As a group, they agreed with the decision, and though the event was days off, they set about planning for the celebration.

Lartha and many of the clan people climbed to the high ground not far from the camp. Maddia, Nasha, and Albo walked beside Lartha to where there was a clear view of the horizon. It was from here that the healer could most accurately note the progress of the sun across the sky.

"I did not notice that the sun moved, except from dawn to sunset," said Maddia. "What makes you think it varies in another way?"

"The simple way is to look where the sun rises and sets every day," answered Lartha. "It is hard to discern the change from one day to another, but with the passage of time, you will see that the sun comes up and goes down in different positions. On the longest day, it sets over there." Lartha pointed to a hill with a rounded top. "On the shortest day, it sets behind the mountain with three peaks."

"Does the moon contribute to our understanding of the seasons?" wondered Maddia.

"Not to my knowledge," said Lartha. "The cycle of the moon is shorter than that of the sun. For each cycle of the sun, there are twelve cycles of the moon."

"How do you keep track of how many moon cycles there are?" said Maddia.

"I have a counting stick. On it, I cut notches for the days of the moon cycle starting from when it is full. In addition, I keep count of the number of cycles. Perhaps it is time that you kept your own moon stick. The next time the moon is full, we shall create a moon stick for you."

"Thank you, Lartha. That is most generous of you," said Maddia. "But tell me more about the sun. You showed me where it sets, but that is not how you track the movements of the sun, is it?" The explanation about the moon stick caused Maddia to conclude that Lartha had a more precise strategy.

"You are too familiar with my ways, child. I use two sticks. They are on that grassy patch." Lartha pointed to a stick that had been pounded into the ground with a rock. It was distinguished by a symbol to confirm that it was Lartha's. No person in the clan would dare to touch it without her consent. A circle of stones surrounded the stick, and alongside it was a smaller stick.

"On many days, I come here at sunset. When the sun reaches the horizon, I note where the first stick's shadow is. I highlight this position with a second stick. When the conclusion of the sun's seasonal journey is at hand, I come daily. That way, I can determine when the season will turn because the shadow will touch the mark I made a year ago on the shortest day."

"May I join you on some days?" begged Maddia. "I want to learn how to trace the path of the sun. Nasha and Albo would love the stroll."

"That would be fine, Maddia. I enjoy your company and that of Nasha and Albo." Lartha stroked both wolves, going from one to the other to share her affection equally. Albo was skittish around many humans, but he was unafraid of Lartha.

Tulio and Griffo were not far away talking with Fong. The toolmaker turned toward Lartha and asked, "Have you decided which stone to use?"

"A stone from over there will do," said Lartha, and she pointed toward a formation of stones at the edge of the high ground.

"It will be difficult, but I have no doubts that we will accomplish it with the assistance of capable men like this." Fong looked at Tulio and Griffo, who smiled shyly. The men of the clan would participate, of course, including the older boys. Tulio and Griffo would serve as assistants to Fong, who would coordinate the relocation of the stones. "Tulio has requested permission to share an idea with you, Lartha."

"Certainly, Tulio. What is on your mind?"

"I heard you explain to Maddia that the sun sets on the shortest day behind the mountain with three peaks. Could we honor the sun by raising three stones? Two would be in front. Beyond them we could put a third stone. On sunset of the last day, the rays would shine through the two stones and strike the third." Tulio hesitated and then continued. "We could wait until sunset to put the third stone in place. That would let us set the sun stone correctly."

The four of them looked oddly at Tulio, not because his idea was foolish, but because it was so grand. The boy had no idea what to say, or whether he should just remain silent.

Lartha looked at Fong and said, "Have you noticed how our young ones have such big ideas? Who would have envisioned that Maddia would enchant a wolf pup, or that Piero would command a herd of aurochs? Is the boy's idea something we can achieve?" From the tone of her voice, they recognized that she thought Tulio's idea was wonderful. Their sun stone would be admired by anyone who saw it.

Fong answered with an amused tone, "He has made three times the work for us, and who knows if we are capable of raising the sun stone in a single day. I have been close to Tulio from when he came into this world, and he has amazed me many times. If the idea is acceptable to you, Lartha, I promise to do my best."

"It is agreeable in many ways," said Lartha. "Let us make it so. Our initial task is to choose the stones."

The stones that they chose were twice as tall as Fong and the width of his shoulders. He and Lartha knew that much of each stone would have to be buried. Besides, they wanted the stones to impress those who saw them, primarily future generations. Fong identified the stones by scratching a symbol into each one with a flint knife.

"We should go to camp at once and tell Baratho what we intend," suggested Lartha. "We shall need the support of many people, yet the daily work of the clan must be completed."

Work commenced the next day. Fong and a dozen of the clan's men and boys dragged the first stone. It was a tedious process because the stones were large and heavy. The ground was soft with moisture, so the footing was poor and the stones could not be transferred easily.

The method the men used was not efficient, but they could think of no less strenuous way to transport such huge stones. They rolled the stones from where they were originally to the site Lartha had picked. A team of men stood beside the stone and pulled it up just a bit. Other men were then able to get their hands under the stone and lift it higher. These actions brought the stone to its side until its weight eventually caused the stone to fall over. The men controlled the descent of the stone so it would not break.

While a group of men conveyed the stone, another dug the three holes. The digging, too, was slow going because the ground was rocky and the only tools they had were shaped stones. The holes had to be very deep, half the height of a man, in order to keep the stones upright. As the holes were made deeper, the men used their spears to loosen the dirt while others removed it with their hands.

It took a day to get the stone to a spot beside its hole. On the final roll, the stone tumbled onto Griffo's spear. The boy was embarrassed that he had not withdrawn the spear ahead of time, and he tried to slip it out without asking for assistance. He did not have the strength to slide it from under the heavy rock, but as he was struggling with the spear, he had an insight.

"Zibio, come here for a moment. Watch the stone while I tug on my spear." Griffo maneuvered his spear while Zibio studied the massive stone. It shifted slightly.

"Do that again," said Zibio. "Wait, let me give you a hand."

The two of them heaved up on the spear, and to the surprise of the men who were present, they raised the stone the width of a hand. It would have taken at least six of the men lifting together to do this.

Seeing what happened, several of the men picked up their spears and forced them under the stone in the same way. With relatively little effort they could turn the stone over.

"That would be difficult to believe, had I not seen it for myself," said Zibio. "Why did we not think of that before?"

"We did think of it before," said Fong. "We just did not think of it now. When we dig up root plants, we perform a similar action. We poke a knife or digging tool into the ground, break up the soil, and then pry up the root with the tool."

"That being true," said Tulio, "then there may be an easier way to convey the stones. When we dig up roots, we thrust the blade into the soil and brace the knife or tool against the ground. You made a special tool for me, Fong. It was like a knife with a longer handle."

Shaking his head, Fong laughed at himself. "It is a good thing we have these young brains to remind us of things. Tulio and I even use the same kind of tool to shift stones in the hearth I built. Let us show you what we mean. Tulio, bring me your spear."

Fong inserted the butt of the spear under the stone. He did not want to use the tip because it might break. He then laid a log that was the thickness of his leg under the spear. He told Tulio to press down on the spear. The boy was able to lift the edge of the stone. The men hoped to try the strategy with the next stone, but it was too late in the day to continue. At Baratho's insistence, they suspended their work and went back to the camp. Around the fire, they told of the struggle they had with the stone and Tulio's brilliant idea.

Chapter 22

The men returned to the stone site in the morning. Motivated by what Fong and Tulio had done, they set to work on the second stone. Using the spear and log routine, they transported the stone more easily. They still flipped it from one side to the other, but the process was faster. By the time they had brought the stone to its place, the sun was high in the sky. They took a break for the midday meal before attempting to raise the first two stones into an upright position.

As they were about to begin, Zibio spoke with Fong. "Remember the day of the children's encounter with the aurochs? We killed an aurochs for food, and as we hauled its body over the spears that were left on the ground, the carcass seemed to slide more readily. I am wondering if the stones could be shifted more easily if we rolled them over spears."

"It would not hurt to try," answered Fong, and he borrowed spears from the men. He put the spears on the ground in front of a stone. He and Zibio used a spear and log to lift the front of the stone, and Griffo put a spear under it. With the stone lying on the spear, two men elevated the rear of the stone, allowing another spear to be positioned underneath.

Following Zibio's directions, Tulio and Griffo knelt down behind the stone. On Zibio's signal, they shoved the stone. It slid smoothly on the spears, which rolled as Zibio had predicted. When the stone reached the third spear, the boys took a break.

Pleased with the efficiency of the effort, Fong said, "We owe Zibio a debt for his memory. Come, let us finish the job, but I think there is an easier way to push the stone."

Zibio borrowed two more spears and handed them to Tulio and Griffo. He instructed the boys to put the butt ends of the spears under the back of the stone and pull up. As they did, the force of their lifting sent the stone forward. With three or four more thrusts of the spears, the stone was by the hole.

"Hold it right there," said Zibio. "Fong and I have to guide the stone."

Standing alongside the stone, Fong and Zibio used their spears to situate the stone more precisely with the hole. They had the boys slide the stone a little at a time over the spears and then had them wait. A pair of men went to the rear of the stone and helped the boys lift it. As they did, the stone dropped into the hole. It was a flawless operation that pleased all of them.

"Our mission is nearing completion," said Fong. "The next step is to raise the stone until it is straight."

The men began pushing the top of the stone. They could do this because most of the weight of the stone was borne by the bottom of the hole. As they forced it upward, Tulio and Griffo put the point of a spear in the ground and the butt of the spear against the stone. This kept the stone from falling backward and crushing the men if they slipped. It was not long before the stone was upright. Baratho and Zibio immediately positioned some rocks in the hole to keep the great stone from toppling.

The alignment of the stone was guided by Lartha, who had been watching the whole time. Maddia and the wolves were with her, and restraining Nasha and Albo was complicated. The wolves thought the men were doing something interesting, and as animals that did things as a pack, they were intent on joining in.

As Lartha got up from the log on which she was sitting, Maddia asked, "How will you determine that the stone is straight?"

Before answering, Lartha withdrew a peculiar rock from a fold in her tunic. Around it was looped a fiber of hemp. She unwound the hemp and showed Maddia how it was tied to the stone. When she gripped the end of the hemp, the stone hung vertically.

"I do not know why it is so, but a stone tied with hemp or other fiber seems to form a perfectly straight line going up and down. With this, I can guide the men as they align the stone correctly."

Lartha walked to within a few feet of the hole where the stone was. She held the hemp and stone at arm's length and had the men shift the stone slightly. She strode around the stone and repeated her assessment of its position. When she was satisfied the stone was straight, the men added small rocks and then dirt to the hole. As they did, they tamped down the dirt every so often by stepping on it and pounding it with the butt of a spear. Packing the dirt and rock mixture in this way made it more likely that the stone would retain its position.

Although it was getting late in the day, the men were eager to work on the second stone. Their experience with the first stone made raising the second stone easier. It went quickly, and once the stone's placement was acceptable to Lartha, everyone returned to the camp in an exhilarated mood.

Two unexpected happenings awaited them at the camp. One was a feast that the men had not expected. At this time of year, there was not much food for the clan. The plants were not producing fruit or seeds, and hunting was less productive because the men were devoting their efforts to the stone monument. The women of the clan had been hunting and fishing, so there was fresh meat. They had also used some of the seeds and dried fruit that had been stored since the growing season. The feast they had assembled was superb.

The other was a secret the women had not shared with the men. While the men had been laboring with the stones, the women had been making strands of hemp using the technique that Belia and Murra had invented. The women had created strands of hemp that were the length of many men and thicker than a child's wrist.

"What is this?" asked Zibio of Belia.

"Maddia told us that you were struggling with the stones. We could not think of anything that would make your work easier. Murra suggested that the hemp strands might be useful, so a group of us made these strands over the last two days."

Zibio replied sincerely, "For now, I cannot think of how they will be of assistance, but we have one more stone to raise tomorrow. We shall bring your strands with us and see how they can make our work easier."

"It is good that we have additional resources," said Lartha, who had overheard Belia's words. "I think that tomorrow is the shortest day. We should do everything we can to erect the third stone before the sun drops beyond the horizon."

Lartha's prediction caused the men to show up the next day with renewed enthusiasm. They wanted to erect the third stone as soon as they could in order to honor the sun and encourage its reappearance. As had countless humans before them, the people of the clan were willing to attempt an extraordinary endeavor despite the risk of failure.

Many of the women, children, and older people came to the site of the sun stone. They wanted to see how the stone would be put up.

The men used their spears to get the sun stone onto flat ground and then lifted it a little. Fong slid two logs under the stone, put a third in front of it, and explained what he was doing. "Yesterday, we had to cover only a short distance, so the spears worked fine. Today, we must drag this stone from here to the hole. I think the logs will roll better than the spears."

Fong and Zibio then acted in a way that the men did not anticipate. They tied the strands of hemp to the stone. The two of them brought the ends of the strands to the front of the stone.

Zibio said, "We are not positive this will work, but we wanted to give it a try. Griffo and Tulio, grab that strand. Ganni and I will use this strand. The rest of you can shove from behind so the stone will advance in the right direction. Pick up each log as the stone advances beyond it. You will have to reposition the logs in front of the stone to keep it going forward."

When everyone was ready, the four of them pulled on the hemp strands. The stone advanced easily because of the logs, and the strands did not break. Those who saw the process were astonished at how well everything worked. As the sun stone was drawn over each log, two men carried the trailing log to the front and put it down so the stone's progress would not be hindered. The men who pushed from the rear were careful to avoid tripping on the log, and the four who dragged it took pains that the stone did not hit the men positioning the log in front.

Hauling the third stone was far easier than either of the previous two had been. The stone seemed to float on the logs, and the coordinated actions of the men were a sight to behold. The crowd that had been watching from afar drew closer to the stone, and the event began to take on the mood of a celebration rather than being an act of labor.

Checo asked if he could be brought to the stone. Leeza and Maddia had described everything to him. He wanted to touch the stone, the logs, and the hemp strands for himself so he could narrate the events later in elaborate detail. The men stopped their effort but remained where they were. Checo walked to the stone, touching it, the logs, and the strands of hemp. He memorized the configuration of the components as well as the name of each worker.

Sensing how well things were going, the women departed for the camp hurriedly. They wanted all of the clan members, including the oldest and youngest, to witness this occasion. The women came back not long after with the rest of the clan and extra food they had brought from the storage baskets. It would be a day the clan would long remember.

In front of the entire clan, the workers dragged the sun stone to the edge of the hole. They drew it over the hole before tipping it in. This time, however, the hemp strands made the job easier and more elegant.

Zibio repositioned the strands on the stone and the process continued. Fong directed the men to use their hands, their spears, and the women's strands to guide the stone into its hole. To those around it, the stone seemed to rise as if by magic into an upright position when pulled by the strands the women had made. Small rocks were dropped into the hole to secure the stone, and it was propped up further with spears.

"We shall leave the stone as it is until sunset," said Fong. "At that time, Lartha will give us guidance as to its final placement." Turning to the women, he praised their effort. "The hemp strands you made were extraordinarily useful to us. When Checo tells this story, he will surely mention how the strands of hemp played a role in creating our monument to the sun."

With the whole clan convened on the high ground, Baratho decided that they should wait here for sunset. It was not too cold, everyone had warm clothes, and because of the foresight of the women, there was plenty of food. An assembly of this kind would be the ideal way to honor the sun.

The time passed quickly, and as the sun approached the mountain with three peaks, Lartha and some of the men made necessary adjustments to the stone. She went behind the stone to check its alignment with the stakes she had put in the ground in the prior year. She directed the men to shift the stone, which they did by prying with their spears. Then, as before, she circled with the hanging stone to confirm that the sun stone was straight. When she signaled her approval, the men filled in the hole with pebbles and dirt, tamping it as they did.

With the sun sinking behind the mountain, the final rays touched the stones. Lartha's arrangement of the stones, in particular the last sun stone, was precise. Just before the sun went behind the mountain with three peaks, its rays illuminated the three upright stones. The sun stone stood out magnificently between the shadows of the two other stones. Tulio's idea succeeded beyond anyone's imagination.

At the moment the sun vanished, the clan set off for the camp in a lighthearted mood while there was still enough light to see. They held a feast by the fire and slept well that night, believing that their celebration of the sun would ensure its return in the morning.

Over time, many travelers would pass by the sun stones. If they were allies and visited the camp of Baratho's clan, they would learn how the stones were raised using spears, rolling logs, and strands made of hemp. They would bring the tale to their own clan, and others would erect stones in a similar way to honor the sun and to celebrate important events. Within a generation, the simple but efficient tools and techniques that the clan developed would spread to humans throughout the world. So, too, would the legend of the girl who enchanted wolves.

Chapter 23

Lartha had been the first to notice that Nasha was changing. It was early spring, and her winter coat was thick. Despite this, Lartha observed that she had put on weight and seemed a little plumper. Moreover, Nasha and Albo had begun digging a den in the side of a hill only a few paces from Maddia's shelter.

"I think Nasha will be having pups in a matter of days," Lartha said to Maddia. "The hole that she and Albo are digging is the den. When it is her time, she will want to be alone in the den."

"Why does she not have her babies in the shelter? That is how the women in the camp do it. Will she and the pups be safe in the den?" Maddia was becoming more dismayed as she spoke.

"Nasha will be fine," said Belia, and she put her hand on Maddia's shoulder. "Having babies is one of the things that female animals are born to do. If we try to interfere, it is likely that we will upset her."

Other than the differences to how she looked, Nasha showed only subtle changes as her time came near. When Maddia joined the gatherers, Nasha went with them. She even hunted with Maddia and the older boys when they were allowed to accompany the men.

Nasha's pups were born under a full moon. Maddia had no question about the timing because it was the first night that Nasha had not slept with her since the day she had brought the pup home. Nasha's head was on Maddia's belly when they fell asleep. When Maddia woke up in the middle of the night, Nasha was not there. She jumped up with her pulse racing, looked around the shelter, and saw that Nasha was gone.

Maddia wrapped herself in the pelt that had covered her while she slept. Wrapped in this warm fur, she tiptoed gently through the shelter so as not to wake her family and stepped into the night. In the moonlight, she saw Albo lying next to the den. She walked over to him and knelt at his side. The white wolf licked her hand, but he did not get up to greet her. Maddia looked inside, but darkness was all she saw.

"I am here, Nasha," whispered Maddia, and she heard a whimper as an answer. The girl drew the pelt around her and sat down with Albo. She fell asleep outside the den beside the white wolf.

A wet tongue woke Maddia. Nasha was licking her face, and Albo was stretching. Maddia assumed that Nasha had given birth, and guessing that she might be hungry, Maddia rose and brought them to the upright sticks on which strips of meat were drying. She fed both wolves and went on a brief outing with them. She gave Nasha a hug before going to the family shelter, and the new mother wolf returned to her pups.

Belia and Zibio had just awakened. Maddia did not want to disturb her brothers, so she whispered to them, "I think Nasha has had her pups."

While the boys slept, the three of them went to see the wolves. Albo wagged his tail when he saw them, but he remained by the den.

"What should I do," asked Maddia.

"There is nothing for you to do," advised Belia. "Nasha is prepared to be a mother." Knowing that her daughter wanted to help, Belia said, "You might feel better if you went into the den and saw the pups. I don't think Nasha would mind."

Smiling brightly, Maddia crawled cautiously into the hole. The light was dim, and the entrance to the den was longer than she had anticipated. When she reached Nasha, she put her arms around the wolf and drew her close. In the faint illumination of the morning sun, she saw five pups. They were nestled together with Nasha. Maddia remembered when Nasha snuggled against her in the same way. Tears of happiness filled her eyes, and she knew that something marvelous had happened.

For many days, the wolf pups did not leave the den. Nasha often went outside during the day, but she did not enter the family's shelter. To no one's surprise, Nasha and Albo were devoted to their babies. Nasha passed most of her time in the den, and Albo waited patiently.

Tulio said that if Nasha were living in the wild, other wolves in the pack would have brought her food. He and Maddia decided that they would ensure that there was enough fresh and dried meat by the den so that Nasha would not be inclined to hunt. Each day, they brought meat to the front of the den. Before they did, they would take Albo for a walk. Though he was a dedicated father, he would have a hard time not eating the food that was left for Nasha.

By the next full moon, the pups were making their way out of the den. They would tumble around with one another by the opening, and they were comfortable with Maddia and her family. This occurred because Maddia looked in on them each day in the den. Maddia would visit with Nasha, and when the wolf left the pups for short periods of time, Maddia would play with them.

The pups became more comfortable on their excursions outside the den. Nasha seemed to recognize this, and on a sunny afternoon, she led the pups to the shelter that was the home of Maddia's family. She prodded them inside, where they sniffed at the interesting new smells. Nasha lay down on the animal skin she had shared with Maddia. The pups came over, nursed for a time, and then curled up for a nap. This would now be their home, too. That night, with Nasha at her side, Maddia slept more soundly than she had in a long time.

With the passing of each day, the pups spent more time exploring the area around the hut. Tulio suggested that Maddia might want to see if the pups were ready to eat fresh meat. They were not, and would eat only meat that Nasha or Albo had chewed and presented to them. After a time, however, the pups would take soft pieces of meat from Maddia and the rest of the family. Lakus liked to impress his friends by holding chunks of meat in his mouth and having the pups nip at them.

All of the clan members thought the wolf pups were a blessing. Nasha and Albo had made the men more capable hunters, and when they traveled with the women on foraging trips, the wolves were very protective. Several families had already volunteered to adopt the pups when they were ready to be separated from Nasha.

Even Gortush and Jartush were interested in the pups. On more than one occasion, they inquired as to how the pups were doing, and when the baby wolves left the shelter to play, the brothers stayed to watch them. Many in the clan judged this to be a good sign, and that the sons of Ushga had at last found a remnant of their father's virtue. Ganni did not believe this in the least, and whenever the brothers were in the vicinity of the pups, he was not far from them.

"Maddia, do not allow Gortush or Jartush to be alone with the pups. I am suspicious of their intentions despite their appearance of interest," Ganni warned.

Chapter 24

"Each of Nasha's pups will trade for countless golden stones," said Gortush. "Her litter will make us richer than any clan in the region. We will form a powerful clan of our own and rule the others."

"We have to find a way to trade with the clans that have the most golden stones. Perhaps we can have the clans bid against one another," declared Jartush. "But first, we must take the pups. It will not be easy."

"I have been thinking of a plan," said Gortush. "We need a distraction, one that will draw the entire clan from the camp. Here is my idea. You will tear down part of the wall that encloses the aurochs. I will tell the clan that the wall has fallen down and the aurochs are stampeding toward the camp. When they go to the stockade, I will take the pups."

"Where will we trade the wolf pups?" wondered Jartush.

"I will meet you on the cliff by the river. I doubt

anyone will think to look for us there when they discover the pups are missing. From the cliff, we will walk down the river. We can trade one of the pups on the way, and when we reach the great water, we can trade those that are left."

The brothers discussed the plan further and became excited about the possibilities. They took special pleasure in knowing that the loss of the aurochs herd would be a hardship for the clan.

Three days passed before the brothers put their plan in place. They wanted it to happen late in the day so they could escape during the night. They picked a time when the moon would be close to full so the evening would not be so dark.

Jartush went to the enclosure and looked for the aurochs. They were far from the wall, so there was little danger to him. He could take a section of the fence down and then make noise to get them to stampede through the gap.

Feeling confident in the plan, Jartush pulled some logs from the wall. They did not come off easily because someone had been fastening the lengths of wood together with strips of leather and hemp. The wall looked flimsy, but it was not, and his frustration grew.

"What are you doing?" demanded a voice from behind him.

Jartush turned quickly and sneered when he saw Piero. "It is none of your business, child," said Jartush. "Return to the camp where you belong."

"It is my business," said Piero. "I am the keeper

of the aurochs. I feed them every day and check that the wall is secure." It had not dawned on Piero that he was in danger, and he was not about to abandon his duties.

Anger got the best of Jartush. He did not want Piero wasting time and interfering with the plan. Taking down the wall was proving to be more difficult than he assumed, and now this boy was badgering him. He spun around and pushed the boy to the ground. The attack was so swift that Piero had no time to prepare. He struck his head on a log and fell to the ground unconscious.

Ignoring the fallen boy, Jartush continued tearing down the wall. Time was running out, and Gortush would at any moment be telling the clan that the aurochs had escaped. Jartush disassembled a section of the wall that was big enough for the aurochs to pass through one at a time. He would have preferred it to be wider, but he knew he must go at once.

Before escaping, Jartush did a horrible thing. He dragged the boy into the stockade. He knew the aurochs would trample him as they broke free. If his plan succeeded in the way he hoped, the clan might think that Piero was responsible for taking down the wall.

In the meantime, Gortush had made his way to camp. He waited a distance away until he thought that his brother would have had time to free the aurochs. When the time was right, he bolted into the center of the camp shouting, "The aurochs knocked

197

down the wall and are loose. They may be coming here." Gortush threw himself to the ground pretending to be exhausted and injured.

Baratho ordered everyone to the enclosure. Before leaving, the women took the smallest children to the shelter of Belia and Zibio. This shelter was chosen because it was large, a rocky outcropping shielded it, and several trees were nearby. If the aurochs stampeded through the camp, they would be unlikely to make their way to this shelter.

Two of the older children, Salora and Reesa, were entrusted with the younger children and the wolf pups. Their mother, Ducatha, hugged them both and told them exactly what they should do. There was food and a skin with water in the shelter, and none of them should come outside for any reason.

The camp was empty except for Gortush and the children. When he was satisfied that no adult member of the clan could see him, he walked into the shelter with the children. Salora and Reesa were surprised to see an adult, but they had no cause to be uneasy.

A group of the younger children were playing with the wolf pups. Gortush ordered them to put the pups in the basket where they slept, which the children did. He put a fur on top of the pups and bent to pick up the basket.

"What are you doing?" asked Salora. "Mother said the pups were supposed to be with us." She was steadfast in her role as guardian of the children and pups.

"I am taking the pups away," stated Gortush. "You stay with the others. Do not provoke me, child."

Something in Gortush's tone worried Salora. "Please," she begged, "do not take the pups. Mother said I am supposed to watch them."

Salora went over to Gortush and put her hand on his arm as he lifted the basket of pups. She pleaded with him not to take them. Gortush swept around and shoved the red-haired girl, sending her sprawling to the ground.

The little children screamed, and Reesa attempted to aid her sister. Seeing her sister rise, Salora insisted that she remain with the children. Tears welled up in Salora's eyes, but she did not cry. Despite being terrified, Reesa backed away and tried to comfort the children.

Gortush scowled at Salora and turned to leave the shelter with the wolf pups. Salora snatched a cutting stone from the floor and hurled herself ferociously at the man. She slashed at his thigh, drawing blood that spilled down his leg. Raging with pain, Gortush slapped Salora in the face, knocking her down once again. This time, she did not try to get up.

After exiting the shelter, Gortush put the basket down. He closed the flap of the hut and stacked heavy pieces of firewood in front of it. Convinced that the children could not leave any time soon, he took up the basket and raced from the camp. He avoided the trails and made his way to the cliff through the woods.

Reesa helped Salora to her feet. She used part of her tunic to wipe a trickle of blood from her sister's lip. The two of them went to the little children and tried to comfort them.

"I must tell mother what happened," said Salora, and she went to the entrance of the shelter. The flap would not move, and she was unable to force the wood aside. Looking around the shelter, she saw no way to get out.

"What about the smoke hole?" asked Reesa.

Salora looked up. The smoke hole in the roof was big enough for her to escape, but there was no easy way for her to get to it.

"I can help you up the shelter pole," said Reesa. "If you stand on my shoulders and hold onto the pole, maybe you can reach the hole."

With Reesa's assistance, Salora was able to clutch the edge of the smoke hole, but she lacked the strength needed to heave herself through it. Seeing this, Reesa put her hands on Salora's feet and pushed as hard as she could. Salora made it through the smoke hole and tumbled down the side of the shelter, hitting the ground with a thump.

Aching from the fall and her bruised face, Salora removed the wood from the front of the shelter one log at a time. She went inside to satisfy herself that Reesa and the rest of the children were unharmed. She found pieces of dried fruit and gave them to Reesa to share with the children. Salora told Reesa that she would return as quickly as possible with their mother and hurried to the aurochs' enclosure.

Chapter 25

Ganni was the fastest runner in the clan, so he was the first to arrive at the stockade. Much of it was intact, but a short section had been pulled down. Undecided about what to do, he waited until the older men arrived.

"Do not make a sound," said Baratho. He and Zibio had caught up with Ganni. They could not see where the aurochs were, and they did not want to startle them. The three of them inched toward the fence quietly and saw a situation that could be disastrous. The aurochs were walking briskly in their direction. They might charge the opening at any moment, and there would not be time to rebuild it.

Ganni was further alarmed to see a figure on the ground. It was Piero, and the injured boy was directly in the path of the aurochs. Getting Zibio's attention, Ganni pointed at his brother, who was just regaining consciousness. The aurochs were nearly upon him, and they had picked up their pace.

Ganni tried to run to Piero, but his father grabbed him. Zibio recognized the gravity of the situation, but he did not want to lose two sons on this day.

Rising to his feet but still unsteady, Piero saw the aurochs coming at him. His recollection of events was fuzzy, and he didn't know how he had ended up inside the compound with the aurochs so close.

Most of the clan was now in sight of the enclosure and could see what was going on. They knew that Piero was in mortal danger, but there was nothing they could do to save him. Not only that, but when the aurochs broke out of the canyon, they might all be trampled.

What happened next stunned those who saw it. The aurochs came to a halt when they reached Piero. The largest animals stood by expectantly. Two of the calves wandered through the adults, came up to Piero, and nudged him. Understanding what they wanted, Piero backed through the gap, being careful not to trip on the logs that had been dislodged. He went to the pile of grass that was beside the wall and threw part of it over. The aurochs commenced eating at once, ignoring the possibility of escaping. Piero climbed up on the wall and hand-fed some of the calves, a practice he had been following for weeks.

Ganni went to Piero's side and fed the aurochs with him. While the animals were distracted, Zibio and Baratho put the fallen logs up to restore the wall. It was not long before the wall was partially repaired, at least to the point where it would fool the aurochs.

The four of them withdrew from the wall to give the animals an opportunity to eat. When they were at a comfortable distance, they asked Piero what had occurred before they arrived.

"Jartush was taking down the wall," said Piero. "I tried to stop him. I remember he pushed me, and I fell. I cannot recall anything beyond that."

"Are you hurt, my son?" asked Zibio. He put his hands on Piero's shoulders and looked him over thoroughly.

"I don't think so," answered Piero, "other than this bump on my head." He rubbed a swelling on the back of his head.

"Why was Jartush taking down the wall?" wondered Baratho, "and how did Piero get inside?"

A distant voice could be heard coming from the direction of the camp. Salora appeared on the trail, and her words were at last understandable. "Gortush has stolen the puppies!"

Ducatha raced to her daughter, who was dirty and breathless. Blood was on the girl's face. "The children, Salora, how are the little children?" asked Ducatha as she hugged Salora.

"They are fine," she replied. "Reesa is with them. Gortush took the basket with the puppies and blocked us in the shelter. I climbed through the smoke hole and came here. We have to get the puppies back." Taking a breath, she proclaimed with a slightly triumphant tone to her voice, "I cut his leg with a tool stone. He is bleeding."

"Let the women go to camp with the children," said Leeza, and everyone approved. Salora did not want to go with them, insisting that she should search for the pups. Her mother persuaded her that she had done everything she could, and reluctantly, the fiery girl with spirit that matched her hair joined the women and went back to camp. Maddia, Nasha, and Albo stayed with the men.

"I think I understand what happened," said Baratho bitterly. "Jartush tore down part of the wall, anticipating that the aurochs would escape. Gortush warned us, believing that we would rush to the enclosure. Their plan was to steal the pups."

Maddia gasped, knelt down, and put her arm around Nasha's neck. Even though she knew otherwise, she was acting as if Nasha understood what Baratho had said.

"They are most likely planning to meet somewhere, but I cannot imagine where." Baratho scanned the terrain, hoping an idea would come to him.

"It must be somewhere they think we would not look," suggested Zibio. "They have stolen the pups for a reason, most likely to trade them. No other possibility makes sense."

"Zibio is right," agreed Baratho. "We should break up into groups of two or three and begin our pursuit. It is late in the day, and if we do not find them soon, we may lose them completely."

Zibio, Tulio, and Albo made their way along a

small trail that wound into the forest. Fresh footprints led down the trail, and they might belong to
Jartush.

Maddia, Griffo, Lakus, and Nasha headed in the
direction of camp. They were to take the trail that
ran parallel to the river. When they got close to
camp, Nasha became agitated. She caught the scent
of something at the edge of camp.

"Gortush took the pups from our shelter," said
Maddia. "Maybe she can track them by their smell."

Looking on the ground where Nasha was poking around, Griffo noticed a dark red stain. "This
might be blood from the cut on Gortush's leg." He
tapped the ground by the spot, and Nasha sniffed
the blood. Now she had two scents to guide her.

With Nasha in the lead, they trotted down the
path, which led them into the woods. "Gortush had
a good plan," said Griffo, "but he never thought that
Nasha would be able to stalk him with such a late
start. He is carrying the pups, so he cannot travel
very quickly. We will catch him before nightfall."

Nasha had no trouble identifying the smell of
her puppies. Every once in a while, she would pull
up, explore the ground with her nose, and whine.
Maddia had to calm her, afraid the wolf would howl
and reveal their location.

"Gortush may be getting tired," said Griffo. "He
is probably putting the pups down when he takes a
break. That is why Nasha is paying such close attention to certain patches of ground."

They could hear the roar of the river on their

left. Griffo was familiar with this area and said they would reach a stream not far ahead. When they did, Nasha lost the trail.

"He went into the stream here," said Maddia. "There are footprints going into the water. We can cross at the same spot and find the scent over there." She pointed across the stream to where it was easiest to climb onto the bank.

Nasha could not, however, pick up the scent on the other side. Suspecting that Gortush had proceeded up or down the stream, they split up. Nasha and Maddia went downstream, while Lakus and Griffo went upstream.

After walking back and forth several times, Nasha located the scent again. Believing that her pups were close by, she bolted from Maddia and bounded up a slope that rose above the river. Maddia was tempted to shout for Nasha but did not want Gortush to learn where they were. She followed Nasha, believing that Lakus and Griffo would figure out where they had gone.

Gortush was at the top of the cliff. He was gripping a spear, and Nasha crouched in front of him growling fiercely. The pups were in the basket behind Gortush.

"Call her off, Maddia, or I will kick the pups into the river."

"Easy, Nasha. We will get the pups." Maddia spoke soothingly to Nasha, and the wolf ceased her growling. She remained tense and looked back and forth from Gortush to the pups in the basket.

The pups had not liked being carried in the basket, and Gortush had to stop often to rearrange them. He kept them covered for most of the trip, but the activity of the pups was pushing the skin up. When they saw Maddia and Nasha, the pups attempted to scramble from the basket.

Troubled by the possibility of losing what he had worked so hard to obtain, Gortush looked away from Maddia and lowered the point of his spear. He bent down to return the pups to the basket and pull the cover over them. Maddia saw this and lunged at Gortush.

Dropping his spear, Gortush stood upright and tried to block Maddia's movement. As he raised his hand to strike her, Nasha attacked him. The force of her jump knocked him backward. The three of them—Maddia, Nasha, and Gortush—tumbled off the cliff and into the river.

Chapter 26

From a distance, Lakus and Griffo saw what happened. Failing to discover any signs of Gortush upstream, the two of them retraced Maddia's steps downstream. They were close enough to the cliff to catch a glimpse of the confrontation, but they were too far away to do anything to help Maddia.

Running desperately, they reached the base of the cliff in time to see Nasha, Maddia, and Gortush hit the water. Lakus grabbed the basket of wolf pups and brought them from the cliff to safer ground. He focused his eyes on the water the whole time. Griffo hurried down behind him but continued past the younger boy to the river's edge.

Nasha was paddling in circles anxiously looking for Maddia when the girl's head popped up from under the water. She coughed and choked for a moment but quickly swam toward Nasha. Seeing that the wolf was unhurt, she glanced in the direction of the shore and saw Griffo waving and yelling. She and Nasha paddled toward him.

Maddia had taken just a few strokes when she saw Gortush floating face-down in the water. Her initial impulse was to let the river carry him away, but she remembered a statement that Lartha had made many years before about being judged by our actions toward others, even those who have wronged us. She grasped Gortush by the hair and brought his head above the surface. She struggled against the current to make it to shallow water where she could stand up. Nasha swam with her the whole time.

Griffo sprinted along the river bank to stay with them, and when Maddia was close enough, he splashed into the water to her side. The two of them dragged Gortush to the shore. He was still unconscious but was breathing.

"Where are Nasha's pups," Maddia asked in a worried tone.

"They are fine," said Griffo. "Lakus is taking care of them."

Griffo pointed to a grassy patch at the base of the cliff away from the river. Lakus was kneeling on the ground beside the basket. He held a piece of leather over the pups and let them nip at it. Seeing the pups, Nasha bolted toward them. Lakus lifted each pup from the basket so Nasha could get closer to them. Their reunion was joyful, and after excited whimpering and licking, Nasha settled herself on the grass and let the puppies snuggle with her.

"Why did you save him?" wondered Griffo. "He

has been nothing but trouble for the clan and may have caused your death. The river would have taken him away forever."

"Lartha's words regarding how we are judged came to mind. I could not fail her or myself. If I allowed harm to come to Gortush, I would be no better than he is. The council of elders will decide what becomes of him."

"How such tolerance came to you I will not ever know," said Griffo. "I hope that if I am ever tested as you were, I will act with equal righteousness." Looking at the figure on the ground, he added, "Gortush has awakened. Let me bind his hands before he does something foolish. We must get to camp as soon as we can so the others will not be worried."

Jartush was far from the canyon. The path he had taken had thick brush and trees on both sides, which made it hard for anyone to see him. He was moving toward the river, but in an upstream direction. He thought that no one would pursue him and that he could continue on the river path to meet with his brother.

Jartush knew the path well because he had used it before to get together with traders from other clans. The path led to a clearing where some trails came together. If Jartush could reach the clearing, it would be more difficult for someone to find him on the next trail if he were being followed.

Arriving at the clearing, Jartush rested for a moment. He was surprised by the sounds of people coming from the river. When they saw him, they acknowledged him cheerily. It was the traders with whom he and Gortush planned to exchange one puppy.

"So, Jartush, you have decided to meet us early. That is considerate of you. Where are your brother and the treasures with which you have tempted us? We have brought the golden stones." The head of the party, Valtar, had not been told what was to be traded, but the brothers had promised him that it would be of exceptional value.

"The special goods are with my brother," responded Jartush. "He is at the place we established. Come, let us join him."

Jartush seemed nervous, and he kept looking down the narrow trail from which he had just come. He tried to hurry them, but the traders wanted to take a break before continuing. They had come a long distance, there was a spring nearby, and they wanted to eat, drink, and relax. From their perspective, there was no urgency.

"No, we have to depart now," announced Jartush, who was clearly upset.

"Is there a problem, Jartush?" inquired Valtar. He was becoming wary of Jartush's behavior. Valtar was a decent man who traded fairly, and Jartush was acting in a way that raised his suspicion.

When he heard a commotion on the trail, Jartush started to run. Two of the traders seized him, not understanding what was happening. They were constraining him when Zibio, Tulio, and Albo got to the clearing.

The men were terrified when they saw the wolf. Tulio knelt down and put his arm around Albo, who was as jumpy as the strangers.

The two holding Jartush let go of him, and he took off down the river trail. Tulio and Albo chased after him, but it was a lopsided contest. With three bounds, Albo was on him. He knocked the man down, and had Tulio not controlled the wolf, he would have killed him. Tulio dragged Jartush back to the clearing, and Albo growled the whole way.

With Jartush once more restrained, Zibio walked up to the leader and the two men exchanged greetings. "Valtar, my friend, you have done us an immeasurable service again. We have been pursuing Jartush and his brother. It is an unfortunate sequence of events that saddens me to tell. And do not be intimidated by the wolf. That is another story, but one that you will enjoy yet have trouble believing."

Zibio knew the trader well because Valtar was from a settlement less than a day's journey away. When Zibio's clan was exiled and had to locate a new home, Valtar's clan consented to share their hunting grounds. It was a kindness that Zibio's clan would never forget. Zibio believed that Valtar persuaded his people that this agreement was a worthwhile idea. Having another clan as a neighbor would benefit both groups because of the possibility of trade. The clans had improved their hunting and gathering skills, so they sometimes had more food and tools than were required for survival. Being able to trade these surplus goods improved the quality of life for everyone.

"We were to meet Jartush and Gortush at the cliff. He promised us that if we brought many golden stones, he would trade for the most wonderful goods of incomparable value. I do not think much of the golden stones," said Valtar, "but they are useful for trading with fools like Jartush. The nest of willow branches that he traded before was worth every golden stone we exchanged. Our women have made many copies. I do not understand how items as worthless as golden stones could be traded for objects as useful as the willow nest."

"You have been of considerable assistance to us," said Zibio. "Let us go to the cliff and search for Gortush. On the way, I will explain about the treasures that he stole."

As they hurried to the cliff, Zibio told Valtar and his companions about Nasha, Albo, and the pups. Jartush was guarded by two of the traders, and Tulio followed behind with Albo. The traders could not believe that such a tale was true, but the proof was the wolf that was with them.

It was not long before they heard voices coming in the other direction on the trail. Seeing who it was, Zibio joined the traders and Jartush, telling Tulio to go ahead with Albo. He did not want the adult wolves to become unsettled by strangers being in the vicinity of their pups. The traders were astounded by what they saw. Two wolves were prancing beside a young girl while a boy carried a basket of pups behind them. It was a scene that no human outside of Maddia's clan could envision.

"When I return home and explain what I have seen and what you have told me, any rational person in my clan will be skeptical. I am glad that I have companions to verify my words." Valtar spoke in a way that reflected his appreciation of Maddia and the wolves. "I am equally glad that our trade with the brothers was not completed. It is likely that they would have deceived us, and we may have wrongly separated the pups from their family."

"We do not know what the future will bring," said Zibio, "but many of us appreciate the wolves and their pups in a way that is difficult to describe. I will speak with Maddia about this, but maybe your clan can adopt one of the pups in a future generation. I trust that she will want to place the pups from the first litter with the people of our clan."

"It would be an honor to have a wolf pup join our clan. If you will allow us, my family and I will visit you and learn from Maddia how to care for the pup," suggested Valtar. "We should be on our way, and undoubtedly, you will want to go to your people. Before we leave, I have a question. What do you plan to do with the brothers?"

"It is not my decision to make," replied Zibio pensively. "The council of elders will issue a judgment. My hope is that the brothers are never given the opportunity to trouble us again."

Chapter 27

The clan's council met to determine the fate of the brothers. Their verdict was that Gortush and Jartush were to be banished. The brothers would be provided with food for several days. They would be conducted to the river, where Valtar would meet them. He and his companions would take the brothers through their territory to the region of a nearby clan with whom they traded, to be escorted to the edge of their land. It would be next to impossible for the brothers to cause trouble for Baratho's clan in the future.

At the same council, another decision was made that would affect the destiny of the clan. The valley would be their perpetual home. The region had enough animals and plants to sustain them, and the aurochs provided a dependable supply of additional meat. Piero's realization that seeds could be used to grow plants wherever they wanted might also prove to be a valuable source of food. Their camp would be rebuilt into a permanent village, and they could avoid the tedious, dangerous trek from one place to another.

Over the succeeding months, Nasha's pups grew quickly. When the time was right, families in the clan adopted them. As had Nasha, the pups became beloved members of the families to whom they were given. Although they were attached to their families, it was always a heartwarming moment when the pups got together with Nasha, Albo, or their litter mates.

Everyone now called the clan's wolves docga. It was the word that Lartha had used when she had originally encountered Albo. The other members of the clan found that the name was fitting because the wolves had brought them so much, mainly the incomparable gift of being needed and loved.

The herd of aurochs was more successful than anyone could have imagined. To the astonishment of the clan, the aurochs seemed content to pass their days in the valley. There were many plants on which they could graze, a stream provided them with water, and the walls of the canyon gave them shelter from harsh weather. Piero and his friends continued to feed the aurochs when it was necessary, and they could even lead the animals to different parts of the canyon where there was better grazing.

With Lartha's help, Piero created a seed collection. He identified the plants the clan was fond of and picked the seeds from these plants. Most of them were grasses with nutritious seeds that could be ground to make cakes. He scattered the seeds where the soil was rich and a dependable water source was available. The plants did well, and he believed that in the future, he could provide the clan with an efficient way to produce most of the food they would need.

On a warm summer day, Leeza made her way to Fong's shelter. He was working behind his hut with Tulio. The stone fireplace, which he called a kiln, was blazing. Fong and Tulio had made an accidental discovery a few days before. When burning embers were mixed with specific rocks, they produced more shiny materials than when they were just heated in the flames. Fong was not sure why, but he was of the opinion that this process was a noteworthy discovery.

"Good morning, Leeza," said Fong in a cheery tone. "What have you brought us today?"

In her hands, Leeza carried an article wrapped in an animal skin. Tulio and Fong interrupted their working as she slowly pulled the covering away. Inside was a clay object that Fong had fired for her the other day. The shape was a sphere with an opening in the top. It was more or less the same size as a person's head. Leeza had created it with clay from the river.

"I wanted the two of you to see this," said Leeza. She held the shape so it caught the sunlight.

Tulio cautiously touched the shape. It was incredible, unlike anything he had ever seen before.

Leeza had painted the shape using the methods that were used in the story cave. The shape had pictures of a wolf, an aurochs, and a boar.

"How can you conceive of these things?" Fong wondered. "Your mind is more visionary than anyone else's. The shape is beautiful, but with the paintings you have done, it is breathtaking." Fong took the shape from her and turned it in his hands.

"You exaggerate as you regularly do, Fong, but I am grateful for your kind words. They are noteworthy because you have worked magic with fire and stones." Leeza had always admired Fong's work, so his praise had special importance for her.

As Fong examined the shape, a party of young people wandered by his shelter. Seeing what was in his hands, Maddia walked to him.

"What have you done now, Fong?" she asked the toolmaker.

"It is not my work," answered Fong, "but Leeza's. She made the object with river clay, and I fired it recently. She just returned to show us how she had painted it to resemble the drawings on the story cave."

The group clustered around and looked at the shape closely. To them, it was a breathtaking sight, one they would remember for the rest of their lives.

Whining sounds from Nasha and Albo let the children know that the wolves did not appreciate being ignored. They had set out on a foraging trip on the high ground that was an easy hike from camp, and the wolves were eager to be on their way.

"You two have very little patience," said Griffo to the two wolves. "Come, we can talk to Leeza about her creation at another time."

Griffo and Maddia led the group to the trail that went up to the high ground. The wolves rambled in front of them, looking back occasionally as if to encourage the humans to hurry. There was nothing the wolves enjoyed more than going for an adventure with the young members of the clan.

The high ground stretched for miles and was covered with a mix of grasslands and clumps of trees. Some of the trees were bearing cherries, which the children had come to pick. As they had done with the figs last season, the children nibbled on the fruit while they filled their baskets.

Maddia threw a stick, which Nasha and Albo chased over and over. Whoever got to the stick first teased the other wolf while bringing it back to Maddia. The dogs played the game until they were exhausted and then came to relax at Maddia's feet.

Griffo was responsible for protecting the children, so his eyes and ears were alert for anything unusual. He heard a faraway sound and said to Maddia, "Listen. I think it is a herd of horses."

The rumble of the hoofbeats caught the attention of the children, and they stopped what they were doing. A cloud of dust in the distance marked the path of the horses. They galloped farther off, and soon they were gone.

"Horses are so graceful," said Maddia, "especially when they run. I have often dreamt about how it would feel to ride on the back of a horse. The sense of freedom must be incredible."

Looking at the girl who had a special place in his heart, Griffo observed, "If anyone ever rides on the back of a horse, Maddia, it will be a person like you."